What the critics are saying…

೫

Nine Gargoyles. "I've always believed the mark of a great author was his/her ability to leave readers wanting more. Jennifer Dunne is a superb author and the ending of *NOT QUITE CAMELOT* will have you shouting "No!" and hastily searching Cerridwen Press for details on book two…" ~ *Safiya Tremayne, In the Library Reviews*

"Think of *NOT QUITE CAMELOT* as a romantic, feminist, anti-Mallory…Did I mention the hot sex scenes?" ~ *Rebecca Salek, Sequential Tart*

"….*NOT QUITE CAMELOT* captures your attention right from the first chapter as we are transported along with Angelique into another time. Jennifer Dunne really brings out the feelings and actions of life in times when no one is trusted and punishment, often for just saying the wrong thing, is meted out regularly. Reynart is a delightful hero who is honorable, sexy and loveable as well as sensitive. Angelique, after some initial confusion, adapts well and is an asset to Reynart. The plot has several twists and turns leading to a surprise ending. While this book is definitely a stand alone novel, the promised sequel will be much anticipated and appreciated." ~ *Elise Lynn, eCataRomance*

"Jennifer Dunne has penned a tale that will have readers wiping away tears or laughing more than once. For a fascinating glimpse into a world long gone, be sure to check out *NOT QUITE CAMELOT*. I can't wait for the next book." ~ *Angela Camp, Romance Reviews Today*

Five cups. "Ms. Dunne has written a lovely story which is the start of a promising series of the adventures of Angelique and Reynart. This reviewer looks forward to each installment." ~ *Cindy Warner, Coffee Time Romance*

Four Lighthouses. "*NOT QUITE CAMELOT* is an interesting fantasy romance. Angie and Reynart make an improbable but believable couple and the author's descriptions of the kingdom; it's customs and inhabitants make the story come alive. ... The palace intrigues and plots make the story very exciting and the plot line moves very quickly." ~ *Moe811, Lighthouse Literary Reviews*

"*NOT QUITE CAMELOT* is an excellent introduction to SHADOW PRINCE. I think Ms Dunne truly has the calling to weave wonderful stories and she didn't disappoint with *NOT QUITE CAMELOT*. I'm greatly looking forward to more stories in the World Gates series." ~ *Cynthia Eckert, Paranormal Romance Reviews*

Four Cupids. "*NOT QUITE CAMELOT* offers a mix of sizzling romance and unique fantasy that is compelling." ~ *Cupid Reviews*

Jennifer Dunne

NOT QUITE CAMELOT
WORLD GATES

Cerridwen Press

A Cerridwen Press Publication

www.cerridwenpress.com

Not Quite Camelot

ISBN # 1419954814
ALL RIGHTS RESERVED.
Not Quite Camelot Copyright© 2005 Jennifer Dunne
Edited by Martha Punches
Cover art by Syneca

Electronic book Publication May 2005
Trade paperback Publication January 2006

Excerpt from *Fugitive Lovers* Copyright © Jennifer Dunne 2005

With the exception of quotes used in reviews, this book may not be reproduced or used in whole or in part by any means existing without written permission from the publisher, Ellora's Cave Publishing, Inc. 1056 Home Avenue, Akron OH 44310-3502.

This book is a work of fiction and any resemblance to persons, living or dead, or places, events or locales is purely coincidental. The characters are productions of the authors' imagination and used fictitiously.

Cerridwen Press is an imprint of Ellora's Cave Publishing, Inc.®

Also by Jennifer Dunne

Fantasy and Science Fiction from Cerridwen Press

Fugitive Lovers

Shadow Prince

If you are interested in a spicier read and are over 18, check out her erotic romances at Ellora's Cave Publishing (www.ellorascave.com).

Hearts of Steel *(Anthology)*

Hot Spell *(Anthology)*

Luck of the Irish *(Anthology)*

Party Favors *(Anthology)*

R.S.V.P. *(Anthology)*

Santa's Helpers

Seasons of Magick *(Anthology)*

Sex Magic

Single White Submissive *(Anthology)*

Tied With a Bow *(Anthology)*

Not Quite Camelot

ঞ

Chapter One
October 17, 1989

"Angie, are you listening to me?" Her mother's tone of voice clearly indicated that she knew the answer was "no" and was not pleased.

Angelique Blanchard reluctantly pulled herself from the pages of her book. They'd left the campus they were visiting late in the afternoon and her parents refused to let her drive the car at night. Now they weren't even letting her read. Marking her place with her finger, she looked up at the front seat of the station wagon. Her mother glared back at her.

"Sorry, Mom. I was reading. What did you say?"

"I said, your father can't see the road with the dome light on. You need to put the book away."

"But Mom, it was just getting to the good part, where Lancelot—"

"Not another word, young lady. Mark your place and put your book away."

Angie stuffed the scrap of ribbon she used as a bookmark securely between the pages, then set the book on the floor along with her empty soda cans and tiny purse. Even though she promised herself every time she went somewhere with them that she'd behave like the mature adult she knew she was, she inevitably found herself acting like a spoiled brat. Reaching up, she snapped off the dome light. "Happy now?"

"Thank you," her father said.

Angie rested her chin on her fist and stared out the window at the rapidly darkening desert. "This whole trip was lame. I told you I didn't want to go to Arizona State."

"Don't start that again, Angie," her mother warned. "It's a good school. And they offer nice financial aid packages."

"I know, I know. The least I could do was go and take a look at the campus. Well, I took a look. And I still don't want to go there. It's totally bogus. A student factory. I want to go someplace small. Someplace where I'll fit in, not get lost."

She had plenty of experience not fitting in during her high school years. Somewhere, she knew, there were teenagers like her, who cared more about the exploits of Robin Hood and the Knights of the Round Table than football, basketball and the latest video game at the mall. The problem had always been finding these mythical kindred spirits. She sensed that her time was running out. College would be her last chance to connect with others like her, while she was still young and carefree enough to enjoy herself.

"She has a point, Janice," Angie's father said. "There's a lot to be said for the personalized attention you get at a smaller school."

Her mother let out a put-upon sigh. "Fine. If you don't care how much the next four years are going to cost, why should I? I won't say another word."

An awkward silence descended over the car, broken only by the soft rush of tires on pavement. Angie stretched out across the back seat, pillowing her head on the armrest, and let the sound lull her to sleep. A series of loud pops startled her, pulling her toward wakefulness.

"Whaa?"

"Go back to sleep, Angie," her father said. "It's just rain."

Fat drops spattered the car, sounding like a kettle of popcorn. The windshield wiper motors whined, sweeping the blades across the windshield at their highest speed.

"Should we pull over?" her mother asked.

"Where? In the middle of the desert? When we get to the next town, I'll pull off."

Angie didn't care about the rain, and would rather get back to that nice dream about visiting Camelot to see Lancelot compete in a joust. She mumbled, "G'night."

"Sleep tight, sweetheart," her mother answered.

Comforted by the familiar refrain, Angie closed her eyes and drifted back to sleep.

* * * * *

Prince Reynart tucked the torn and bloody sleeve of his practice tunic against his side as he stalked through the lesser used corridors and stairwells of the castle toward his suite of rooms. He couldn't allow any agents of the Queen to see the proof of his unchaperoned sparring, especially since it was her precious son Reynart had been sparring with. She'd run to the King, claiming the sparring without a mage present was a plot to assassinate Alaric and make it look like an accident, foiled only by her son's superior skill with a sword. Never mind that if Reynart wanted to assassinate his younger half-brother, Alaric, he would already be dead. He couldn't risk the King possibly believing her.

The measured tread of two pairs of boots sounded from around the corner. There weren't supposed to be any guards patrolling this corridor during the afternoon, only servants hurrying about their duties. That's why he'd come this way.

Reynart ducked into the nearest room, pulling the door closed but not latched behind him. His ears strained to chart the course of the two guards in the corridor, as his gaze searched the dim room for further hiding spaces. Spindly chairs lined the walls and no concealing drapes softened the embrasures that narrowed to arrow slits before widening to hold windows in the castle's outer wall. The room's single large piece of furniture was a shrouded harpsichord in the far corner.

He bit his lip to keep from swearing, and summoned the calm he'd learned to depend upon in battle. The music room was forbidden to him, as music was one of the pastimes that might distract him from mastering the arts of war. His back throbbed with the memory of his last warning, when he'd dared to ask a minstrel for details about his music. Painful as the King's warning had been, at least he'd lived through it, unlike the minstrel. There would be no such leniency if Reynart disobeyed the King's direct order a second time.

His breath stilled as he settled into a trance-like state of waiting. He had no way of predicting if the pair outside were honest soldiers who might be sympathetic to his position, members of the King's fanatical elite guard or men who curried favor and gifts by reporting to the Queen. He called to mind the faces of all the guards he knew he could trust, so that he would recognize them instantly. If the guards entered the music room, he would have but a moment to decide whether or not to attack them. Should they prove to be enemies, with surprise on his side, he could overpower them both without killing them. They would not dare to report his whereabouts when they woke, since it would require them to describe their own failures.

He released a dagger into his hand, turning it so that he could strike with the pommel, and crouched in readiness. But the steady boot treads passed by the music room and continued down the corridor. The guards were not searching the rooms, merely using the supposedly deserted hallway as the fastest route to wherever they were going. Reynart's breathing returned to normal as the guards' footsteps faded to silence.

Stowing the dagger in his wrist sheath, he fled to safety. He slipped out of the music room, silently closing the door, and hastened down the hallway. Rounding the corner out of the private wing, he came upon a young lady in a heavy blue court dress, gazing in confusion at the crossing of two corridors as she turned slowly in place. Reynart halted abruptly, turning his injured arm away and tensing against the possible threat of a person who didn't belong here.

As her slow turn brought her around to face him, her eyes widened and a breathless cry of surprise escaped her lips. He quickly assessed the fine wool and velvet of her embroidered blue gown and her elaborately braided blonde hair, placing her as minor nobility. Judging from the soft curves of her face and her slight build, she was likely about sixteen, on her first visit to the castle and hopelessly lost. The guards who had almost caught him had no doubt been summoned to search for her. She was too pretty to be allowed to wander the halls unescorted.

"Good afternoon, milady. May I aid you to find your way?"

She glanced to either side, as if a landmark might suddenly appear, rendering his assistance unnecessary. A slight crease marred the smooth perfection of her forehead as she frowned. "I have no idea where I am. The last thing I remember is falling asleep in the back seat of the station wagon. Maybe I'm dreaming you."

The young woman gazed at him with a warm smile, while Reynart tried to puzzle out her words. She seemed to be saying she'd arrived in the back of a wagon from one of the outlying guard stations. Yet no noblewoman would travel so. Perhaps she was a foreigner from one of the recently conquered provinces and the strain of getting lost on her first day at court was making her less than skillful with her words.

Whatever the girl's difficulty, they couldn't stand here in the corridor while they discussed it. The family wing behind him might be off-limits to courtiers, but this was a public hallway. Someone else would walk past soon and her chances for an advantageous marriage would be destroyed if a courtier found her in secret conversation with the Bastard Prince.

He inclined his head. "Allow me to lead you to a quiet room where you may gather your thoughts and refreshments may be summoned if you desire them."

The kitchen servants would not betray him. He'd spent too many years hiding among them when the King had cast him out for some failure or other. Most would keep silent out of loyalty to him, and well-earned fear would hold the others' tongues.

A broad grin burst across her face like a beam of sunshine. "Let's get out of this hallway so I can stop blocking traffic, you mean? What the hey. May as well let this play out. Lead on, Macduff."

"My name is Reynart." He knew of no Macduff in the castle. It sounded vaguely like a mountain name. Was that where she was from? It would explain her strange manner.

"And my name is Anjeli." She pronounced it with a strange clicking at the end.

He glanced over his shoulder at her as he led her to the empty morning room, with its soothing view of the rose garden. She walked slowly, kicking the heavy folds of her gown out of her way, until she finally grabbed the fabric in both hands and lifted the skirt away from her feet to hurry after him.

She had not reacted to his name. He expected that a newcomer might not recognize him, especially dressed as he was in the torn and bloody tunic and covered with dust from the practice field. But in the last eighteen years, the name Reynart had been considered ill-omened and it hadn't been very popular before his birth. The only Reynart in D'Altha Castle, in fact in the entire city of Dalthar, was King Ulrich's bastard. Even the most far-flung subject in Nord D'Rae would recognize the name. Yet she showed no reaction.

His mind spun with possible explanations, each more unlikely than the last, as he guided her to a seat in one of the overstuffed chairs with a view of the gardens, her back to the door. It would also completely hide her from the casual view of anyone passing by in the corridor outside.

"Would you like anything to eat or drink?"

"No, thank you." She reached up and caught his hand. "Please, stay and explain this place. Am I in Camelot?"

Reynart stared at her hand resting upon his. No one ever laid a hand on him, save the occasional warrior's clasp after a well-fought battle. Honorable people were distanced by his position, and the dishonorable feared his skill with the knife. Even his sister had refrained from offering comfort after he reached his fifteenth year and the King had declared him too old to be coddled. He suddenly realized how much he missed simple human touch.

She also stared at her hand resting upon his. "You feel warm and alive, not like a dream at all."

Being in the royal castle might be a dream come true for her but her words reminded him that this was neither the time nor place for dreams. Not for him. He reluctantly slid his hand out from beneath Anjeli's. His family tormented him enough. He did not need to add to his suffering by torturing himself with reminders of things he could not have.

Sitting in the chair facing hers, he said, "You have wandered into the private wing of the castle. The rooms on this floor are used as audience chambers for informal meetings."

She tilted her head and smiled. "Like ours?"

Reynart felt his lips turning up to return her smile, and forced his face to an appropriately stern expression. "I am hardly in a position to grant audiences."

"No? Don't you belong in this wing either?"

Her unexpected blow struck through his defenses. He had laid claim to his rooms upstairs for the past four years, the longest he had ever remained in the King's graces. But he and everyone in the court knew that at any moment, he might say or do something to enrage the King and find himself cast out. Again.

A cutting remark sprang to Reynart's lips, one of the three dozen ripostes he'd used so often that their delivery was as polished as any of his dagger strikes or sword thrusts. Yet the words remained unsaid.

No tightening of the smooth skin around Anjeli's eyes or lips hinted at eager anticipation of his disgrace. No malice glittered in her wide blue eyes. In that moment, he realized she was truly innocent of who he was and his situation in the court.

Reynart's breath caught in his chest. She knew nothing about him. He might talk to her, as any man might speak to a lady, without his reputation coming between them. She was actually talking to him, to Reynart, not fencing words with the Bastard Prince.

For just a moment, he imagined not telling her. But she would learn the truth sooner or later. Better she hear it from him now, than have reason to believe he had betrayed her trust. He could live with her fear of him. It was no less than he expected. He did not want her hatred.

"It would not be to your benefit for me to entertain you," he said slowly, searching for the right words. "My position in the King's court is precarious. If we were discovered speaking to each other in private, when the King had not given us leave for the meeting, there are those who would ever after question your loyalty. No nobleman would marry you, lest the contamination spread to him as well."

She blinked. "I'm seventeen years old! I won't be getting married for years and years."

"If you are not seeking a husband, why have you come to court?"

"It wasn't my choice." She frowned, her gaze turning pensive, then shook her head as if to dismiss unpleasant thoughts.

"Your parents wish you to wed and you do not?" He recognized Ladria's complaint. However, his half-sister was a mage. Not even the King would force her to marry against her will.

"No, they don't want me getting married either. Well, I mean, they do, but not now. Not until after I finish college."

"You are going to a collegium?" Reynart leaned forward with interest, his torn sleeve flapping as he shifted position. "Where? Are you training to be a bard or a mage?"

"At least you're not pushing Arizona State." She tilted her head, her brow furrowing, as she considered his question. "Go to college to learn magic? I suppose Merlin and all the rest had to learn it somewhere. The books skip over that part. But as for my plans, I haven't decided where I'll be going yet. We have to figure out the finances."

Reynart let pass her first comment, attributing the strange saying to a mistranslation. Instead, he focused on the rest of what she'd said. He'd never heard of any Merlin at court. Perhaps he was her village's mage. If she was reading his books of magic, she must be well advanced and would certainly be accepted at one of the mages' collegiums. Provided she could afford the entrance fees.

"You are seeking a patron to sponsor you?" He could arrange that. For his sake, Ladria would cheerfully write a glowing letter of recommendation. If Anjeli was willing to wait until his sister's return, she could attend any mages' collegiums she desired. More importantly, as a mage, Anjeli would be an independent woman, uninjured by association with him.

Her expression clouded. "I'm seeking a place I belong."

"Again, milady, I offer my assistance. Only tell me how I may aid you."

Anjeli gave an unladylike snort that charmed with its complete lack of affectation. "It seems pretty far-fetched to ask a dream for college admissions advice."

"Where are you staying while you are in Dalthar?"

"I… Dalthar? This isn't Camelot?"

"No, milady. I regret that I do not recognize the name, though you have mentioned it twice. Is that the property of the lord or lady you came to court with?"

An insane thought occurred to Reynart. If she was imposing upon some distant relatives in the city for her lodgings, he could offer Anjeli rooms in the castle. They had plenty of guest rooms for visiting dignitaries, and even some lesser rooms for those dignitaries' staff. Surely someplace could be found for her.

Except she was studying to be a mage. The King would not wish him to associate with her. Becoming friendly with any mage other than the odious court mage, Gervaise, or one of the army's sworn mages, would be seen as an attempt to establish his own independent power base, a threat the King would not hesitate to put down. A letter of sponsorship could be forgiven, or at least excused, especially if it was actually penned by Ladria. Actively spending time with Anjeli, however, would be neither forgiven nor excused.

Reynart stiffened, remembering past punishments the King had meted out. He had no wish to visit the dungeon again.

"Where did you—?" He broke off his question and held his finger to his lips, urging Anjeli to silence while he listened carefully. Two sets of heavy boots were traversing the corridor. They moved slowly, stopping frequently. The guards had come back and were checking individual rooms.

Anjeli stared at him out of wide eyes. He didn't know what had startled her, the possibility of discovery or seeing Reynart's shift into assassin mode. Whichever it was, she had the sense to remain silent. If the guard found her with him, her chances of finding a patron to support her studies would disappear and even Ladria would not be allowed to help her. Assuming she lived through the King's inevitable questioning, which was by no means guaranteed. As long as Anjeli stayed quiet and out of sight, Reynart could best protect her by hurrying the guards on their search.

He confirmed that she would not be visible from the door and that he would be. After tucking the worst of his tunic's bloodstains out of sight, he shifted his posture so that his wounded arm was shielded by his torso, then leaned back in an attitude of casual rest and composed his features in the stone-faced expression he used at all public occasions. Hopefully, even if the guards were spies for the Queen, they'd be too intent on their search for Anjeli to take much notice of Reynart's condition.

A moment later, the door opened and a guard looked inside. He spotted Reynart and straightened, slapping his palm to his chest in salute. "My lord Prince."

"Were you looking for me?"

"No, my lord Prince. We're looking for a woman who snuck into the castle."

"Past the gate guards?" Reynart lifted one eyebrow, filling his voice with disdain. He recognized the men as guards who were loyal to his brother and, thus indirectly, to the Queen. They couldn't be allowed to see his injury and the best way to get rid of them was to attack. "Does my father know of this?"

"Uh, no, my lord Prince. That is, she didn't sneak past the gate guards. She was with Gervaise and somehow he let her loose to wander the castle."

"The court mage is keeping prisoners now? Or have the castle guards been deputized to oversee that wretch's paramours?"

"Neither, my lord Prince. Gervaise says the woman is dangerous. He was treating her for some magical ailment and had not completed his treatments when she escaped. None of us wants unknown magic loose in the castle."

"The King would not like that," Reynart agreed.

The guard smiled and nodded, reassured that they had resolved their misunderstanding. "So, have you seen her? She is probably strangely dressed and may speak a strange language."

Reynart's eyebrow lifted again. "You don't know? Gervaise was not very forthcoming with his description, was he?"

"She's a foreigner. Depending on how confused she is, she may not remember to speak our language. And the clothing she wore when she escaped was strange but she may have stolen a disguise since then."

Reynart didn't need to look at Anjeli hiding in her chair to know she was the woman the guards were searching for. But he was not letting Gervaise have her. The mage had no concept of altruism. Removing a curse from an unimportant noblewoman, when he had not been explicitly ordered to do so by the King, ran counter to every self-indulgent habit the mage possessed. And if the King had taken a personal interest in Anjeli, the guards would be too fearful of his wrath to waste time explaining anything about the situation.

No, it was far more likely that, rather than curing her, Gervaise had captured Anjeli with the intent of placing his own spell upon her. Given the girl's obvious beauty, Reynart had few doubts about the nature of the enchantment Gervaise intended.

"I see why the guard was summoned, then. Aside from her other qualities, the woman is a thief."

The guard's eyes widened. Apparently, this was the first time he'd realized a woman likely to steal clothing would be equally likely to steal other things, things it was his job to protect. Alaric's patronage would count for nothing if the guard failed at his duty.

Reynart gestured with his good arm at his dust-covered tunic. "Your missing woman did not find her way down to the practice field. If I come across the woman you described, I will call a guard to take her back to Gervaise. You may return to your search and not bother me again."

"Yes, my lord Prince." The guard saluted again and bowed out of the room, closing the door behind him. Reynart held up his hand, commanding Anjeli's silence, until the sounds of the guards' boots faded into the distance.

He looked at her for the first time since the guard had come in with his outlandish story. She had compressed herself as small as physically possible, making her wide blue eyes seem even more huge in her death-pale face. Her fingers worried blindly at the ribbons edging her sleeves.

"Things don't take you by surprise in dreams. They can scare you, but they can't surprise you. No matter how weird it is, you just accept it in a dream. Those guards, and your reaction, surprised me. This isn't a dream, is it?"

"No, milady. Much as I have often wished otherwise, this is real."

She shook her head. "I shouldn't be here. They know that. That's why they're looking for me."

"I know."

"You knew? Then why didn't you turn me in?"

Reynart smiled softly, naturally falling into the manner used with skittish horses. The last thing he needed right now was for Anjeli to panic and bolt.

"I will not turn you over to the guard, nor to Gervaise. I promised to inform them if I found someone matching their description—oddly dressed and speaking a strange language. You are quite properly gowned as an unmarried noblewoman should be, and speak the common tongue."

Anjeli uncoiled, her hands falling still in her lap, but her eyes were still too wide and her face too pale. "I don't remember anything about a magician. I remember my life with perfect clarity, right up to falling asleep during a rainstorm. Then I was standing in the hall where you found me. You were the first person I saw."

Reynart shook his head. "That is not possible. The castle is protected by layers of magical defenses to prevent people from entering by magic."

"None of this is possible!" Anjeli sprang to her feet and paced nervously, occasionally stumbling as her legs tangled in her skirts. She pinched her arm, repeatedly, then came over and laid her hand along his cheek. "But I'm not asleep. And you're real."

The touch of her soft hand on his skin scattered his wits and he said the first thing that came to mind. "You are not used to wearing such heavy skirts?"

"No. That's why they keep tangling me up. I'm used to jeans—uh, I guess you'd call them trousers—and if I do wear a skirt, it's a miniskirt." She made slicing motions with her hand a few inches above her knees. At first he only noted that her delicate fingers no longer cradled his jaw and then he realized with shock that she was indicating the length of her skirt.

"You let men see your legs?"

Her forehead creased. "They're just legs. It's not like I'm letting my ta-tas hang out."

The words were unfamiliar but her meaning was clear. He imagined the laces of her gown undone, the bodice pushed off of her shoulders and her ta-tas, as she named them, exposed to his gaze, to his touch. His palms itched to cradle the weight of her breasts. Considering how soft her fingers had been, the hidden skin of her breasts would be as smooth as the finest silk.

He swallowed, his fingers twitching as he pictured the flesh of her areolas puckering like the nubby rasp of raw silk. Resting atop their silken beds, her nipples would rise and harden like ornamental buttons carved of carnelian.

Heat filled his loins, lifting his spear for an opening sortie. He shook his head, hoping to clear it. It didn't help.

"You are unfamiliar with our ways and cannot simply wander the halls. The guards would soon find you and betray you to Gervaise. You need a place to hide."

"Can you hide me?"

She gazed at him with complete trust and faith. Captivated by that gaze, Reynart felt his heart tremble and knew in that instant that he would willingly die for this woman, to preserve her faith in him. He prayed it would not come to that.

"For now, you may find safety in my rooms. None may enter them without my permission, so you need not worry about the guards discovering you. When my sister returns, she may be able to assist you. She is a skilled mage. Not as powerful as Gervaise, but she makes up for it with more knowledge."

"When will she return?"

"Unfortunately, that I do not know. She is visiting her uncle's court and will stay until she wears out her welcome."

"Her uncle?" Anjeli's brows furrowed. "Not your uncle?"

"No." Reynart took a deep breath. He had hinted around his status long enough. Anjeli deserved to know the truth of who he was. "Ladria is my half-sister, born to the first Queen. Just as Alaric is my half-brother, born to the second Queen."

"Your mother was the third Queen?"

"My mother was maid to Ladria's mother."

"I'm inside Alice's looking glass. Everything's backside front and bottom-side up," she muttered. Reynart was still trying to puzzle out her meaning when she said, "However I got here, it's important I understand. And I don't. The guard called you Prince. How can you be a prince when…?"

Her cheeks colored a delightful shade of rose and her gaze dropped to the floor.

"When I am a bastard, born to a lowly maid?"

Anjeli nodded, still looking at her feet.

"I do not know how it is where you are from but, in Nord D'Rae, the royal line must be bonded to the magical gate energies at birth in order to control the kingdom's gateways. Ladria could not be bonded, because of her mage gifts. The King needed an heir, the Queen was dead and I was handy." He shrugged. It was so simple when he explained it like that, concealing so much of the painful reality he lived in now.

"But when he remarried…?" She glanced up quickly, before coloring and ducking her head again.

"When Alaric was born, many of the King's counselors urged him to…disinherit me." Reynart sidestepped the detail that the only way to break a gate energy bonding was by killing the person who was bonded to the gate. "He decided instead that I could serve a more useful purpose as a goad to Alaric's good behavior. He was to do as the King wished or I would inherit instead of him."

Over the years, the King's original plan had shifted so that now Reynart stood to inherit the kingdom, unless he angered the King. Or unless one of the Queen's many schemes to restore her son to preeminence succeeded.

Anjeli lifted her head, fire sparking in the depths of her eyes. "That's terrible! Normal sibling rivalry is bad enough but to encourage it that way is insane. What did he think he would accomplish?"

Reynart froze, shocked by her words, until he realized she knew nothing of the King's legendary rages. "Do not criticize the King, milady. Ever. Even if you think you are alone in an empty room. His anger is not gentle."

He shuddered, imagining Anjeli's torn and bleeding flesh, her beautiful face distorted by screams of pain and terror. She must not end up in the King's dungeon.

Locking gazes with her, Reynart leaned forward and clasped her cold fingers. "Promise me, milady. Promise that, for as long as you are in this court, you will speak no word against the King, or Alaric, or the Queen."

"I…I promise."

Reynart would have pulled back but her fingers tightened on his, trapping his hands in her grasp. She turned his hands palm upward, studied them briefly, then released his left hand so that she could trace the sword calluses on his right. Her fingertips whispered over the ridges of hardened skin like a butterfly in a field of flowers, lighting briefly then moving on.

He didn't know what truth she hoped to read in his palm, and didn't care. He only wanted her to continue touching him, forever.

Angie stared at the warm hand she held in hers, tracing the tiny scars and picturing the hilt of the sword that had toughened the skin in such an interesting pattern. She looked around the room again, noticing the intricate carving on the chairs and detailed stitching of the wall hangings, then glanced out the window to the garden where rose bushes bloomed profusely in every shade of pink, white and gold. It was real.

She fought back an urge to start screaming, terrified that once she began, she'd never stop. It was insane. Impossible. She must be dreaming. And yet she couldn't argue with the truth of her senses. She was not sleeping in the back of the car. She was here.

And here, wherever it was, was not safe. The mysterious Gervaise seemed to have summoned her here for some nefarious purpose, although fortunately she hadn't arrived where he'd expected. She'd read enough tales of the Round Table to recognize Gervaise as an evil sorcerer, perhaps a male Morgan LeFey. Although by Reynart's recent confession, he'd then be Mordred, the king's bastard, and that didn't sound at all right. He acted more like Lancelot, rescuing Guinevere. That's how she'd think of him, as her Lancelot, even though he looked more like Richard Grieco, with the same intensity and dangerous attitude. But just like Booker on *21 Jump Street*, he'd only be dangerous to the bad guys.

Her fingers tightened around Reynart's, her anchor of chivalrous stability in this confusing world. "If you're going to hide me, we should probably go as soon as possible."

Just as he had the first time she clasped his hand, he stared at her fingers wrapped around his with a look of wonder, as if it was beyond imagination that someone would hold his hand. He'd caught both her hands and held them when he sought the promise about not bad-mouthing the royal family, but that wasn't the same. His grip had been more of a method of focusing her attention forward, on him, for her promise. The way she held his hand now was a gesture of trust and an offer of friendship.

Some remembered pain darkened his green eyes and he deftly slid his hand from her grasp, refusing her offer. "Follow me. Stay quiet."

Angie hiked up her skirts and followed him into the hallway. Even in boots, he walked without making a sound. She tried to step as softly as she could, walking on her toes, although the thin leather slippers on her feet did nothing to protect her from the hard stone floor. She winced silently, certain that the balls of her feet would never forgive her.

They reached the intersection where she'd first appeared and turned down one of the side corridors. It dead-ended in a flight of stairs. Reynart went first, beckoning her upward when he reached the landing and could see that the way ahead was clear.

He waited for her at the top of the stairs, leaning down to whisper in her ear as she drew level with him. "Stay here. I need to see how many guards are in the hall."

His whisper had been barely louder than a breath and she knew she could never answer as quietly. So she simply nodded.

He shot her a brilliant smile that left her so stunned, she never saw him disappear down the hall. Good Lord, the Prince was gorgeous! She'd known he was good-looking, of course, even though his black hair was spiky with sweat and his face and clothes were covered with a fine layer of dirt. He moved with an innate grace and the sense of tightly leashed power. But all the time he had been speaking to her, his expression had been focused and contained, making it clear that, while Reynart might be helping her, he did so for his own reasons and those reasons had nothing to do with liking her or caring for her. That smile, however, lit up his eyes so that they looked like faceted emeralds sparkling in the sun and transformed the sharp edges of his cheeks and jaw into a prism that reflected the jewels' light. It made her believe that anything could be possible. That he might not just be *a* Prince, he might be *her* Prince.

Chapter Two

Reynart strode down the corridor toward his rooms, surreptitiously angling his body to hide his wounded arm as he pretended to adjust his belt. Only one guard, at the end of the hall by the King's rooms. A formality, indicating none of the members of the royal family were in their chambers. Unfortunately, the guard was not one that he trusted.

He frowned as he opened the door to his chambers, automatically reaching inside the partially opened door to disable the crossbow trap before it fired a bolt at his heart. Alaric had run from their practice bout after wounding him. He expected his brother to have returned to his rooms.

A year ago, he could have said why his brother ran, and where he'd gone. He didn't think Alaric would carry tales of their forbidden duel to the Queen, or Heavenly Pair forbid, the King. Their relationship had changed since the summer wars, but not by that much. Still, it bothered him, one more symptom of the gulf yawning between them.

Reynart hurried through the sitting room to the bedroom beyond. Pulling off his shirt, he winced as the fabric stuck to his wound ripped free. He tossed the shirt into the basket of mending that was beginning to grow to alarming proportions, then wet a cloth from the ewer by his bed and cleaned the wound. As he'd thought, it was little deeper than a scratch and needed no other treatment. A second pass of the cloth wiped the dirt of the practice field from his face and hair.

He selected another shirt from his armoire, a blue as close to the color of Anjeli's dress as he could find, pulled it over his head and left his chambers without resetting the trap. He and Anjeli would need to get into the room as quickly as possible. Or at least, she would—he'd need to time his approach carefully so that the guard saw him, but only him, opening the door and entering the room.

His initial plan, to simply inform the guard that he was taking a woman into his chambers, would not work. Not with the guards on the lookout for a missing woman, and a guard of dubious loyalty watching the hall. He'd have to fall back on his secondary plan, sneaking in when the chambermaid came to light the fires in the royal suites. The guard's primary purpose was to protect the King's chamber. He'd have to supervise the chambermaid when she was in there. That would give Reynart and Anjeli approximately half a minute to get from the stairwell to his door.

He walked slowly down the corridor, as if his whole purpose in returning to his chambers had been merely to clean up after sword practice. He turned the corner into the stairwell and found Anjeli pressed up against the near wall, the last place someone would look as they came around the landing. It wasn't much of a hiding place—the castle had been designed to create the minimum number of hiding places possible—but it showed a surprising amount of intelligence given the nonsense she'd been speaking earlier.

As always when things surprised him, his suspicions rose. She was obviously clever. Clever enough to pretend not to know who he was? Was she perhaps working with Gervaise, in some plot to discredit him? He knew the mage favored Alaric over him, since Alaric indulged the mage's base desires, while Reynart found the mage repulsive. Of course, given the man's magical prowess, perhaps it was for the best that he allowed himself to be so easily distracted by serving girls and chambermaids. If he ever managed to remain completely focused on his magic, he would be truly dangerous.

In fact, the girl before him looked remarkably like Gervaise's preferred type, except for being a member of the nobility. She was young, slender and athletic, with a modest cleavage showed to full advantage by her tightly laced bodice. And after all, the only reason he assumed she was a member of the nobility was her appearance. Her manners were nothing like those of the young women of the court. She was quite possibly nothing more than someone's servant dressed up as a noblewoman.

However, as Gervaise would certainly know, he could not afford to take that chance. He would see her to safety first. Then he would find out who she was and what she was doing here. And this time, he would have the truth.

If she was truly innocent of who and what he was, he would kill anyone who tried to harm her. But if she was only pretending innocence, he would kill her himself.

* * * * *

Angie instinctively shrank further against the cold stone wall, alarmed by the menace radiating from the Prince. He'd washed up and changed his shirt, now wearing a loose tunic of deep blue, with brilliant green embroidery around the cuffs and open collar. The clean clothing should have made him seem more civilized. Instead, the loose sleeves called attention to the black leather vambraces sheathing his forearms, reminding her that he was a warrior. And at the moment, he looked more than ready for battle.

A distant bell tolled, the sound carrying faintly through the opening in the wall. Remembering how ringing church bells historically accompanied funerals, she didn't think it was a good omen. But Reynart seemed pleased, his lips curling in an evil smile.

"We wait," he whispered. "Quietly."

He positioned himself so that he could be clearly seen from the stairwell, but not by anyone in the corridor beyond. This put Angie behind him and he repeatedly glanced over his shoulder at her while they waited in tense silence, as if he thought she might have disappeared since he last checked on her. Then again, thinking back on their last conversation, he clearly believed that she was going to school to become a sorcerer. Sorcerers might well be able to appear and disappear at will.

She tried to focus on her situation, on the evidence that was accumulating that this place was real and not a dream. But if that were true, then she might be stuck here. Her pulse pounded and she panted in shallow, raspy breaths as the details of the world around her turned fuzzy and gray. She didn't belong here. She had to get home again. Her parents would be worried about her.

Instinctively, she stepped away from the wall. Reynart turned to face her, a knife in his hand, before she could take a second step.

Her heart thundered and she stopped breathing entirely. Trembling, she froze in place, her eyes locked on the gleaming blade in his hand.

He lowered his arm, the blade returning to whatever concealed location it had come from, and glared at her. "Wait quietly and don't move," he reminded her, his soft whisper barely carrying the few feet that separated them.

Wordlessly, she backed up, until the wall smacked her shoulder blades. He frowned at the additional noise, but then turned his back on her again.

Gradually, her fear faded, replaced by a strange, buzzing awareness of the man in front of her. Even though she was a senior in high school, her school had three times as many girls as boys, so she'd never had a boyfriend. She had a general idea of what went on at make-out parties or in the backs of cars. From what other girls said, giggling at their lockers, it seemed to involve a lot of awkward fumbling.

She knew that Reynart would never be awkward. He'd be intense, graceful and dangerous, like a tiger who allowed you to stroke his fur. The knowledge that he might lash out with his deadly claws at any moment only added to the thrill.

Kissing him wouldn't be like kissing one of the slobbering boys at her school. He'd be cool, calm and totally in control as he claimed her mouth. Or maybe as he claimed more than her mouth.

A vague itch spiraled deep within her, making her long to shimmy and rub herself against the hard wall to satisfy the aching need for pressure against her skin. Mindful of Reynart's warning, she forced herself to remain still. But rather than dissipating, the ache grew, until it was a struggle not to fidget. She pictured his hard thigh, clad in his skintight black leather pants, thrust between her legs while she rubbed up and down against him.

She choked back a whimper of desire, earning her another glare. There was no reason to antagonize him. He'd done nothing to indicate he was attracted to her, behaving with simple courtesy, confusion or tightly leashed anger. There'd been no sighing, no declarations of her beauty, none of the signs of courtly romance she'd learned of in her books. Then again, he was taking her to his rooms. That had to mean something.

A scuffing footstep upon the stairs interrupted her musings. She cringed against the wall, trying to make herself smaller. Before her, Reynart tensed, the knife again appearing in his hand.

A girl, wearing a simple brown gown and carrying a basket of kindling that was obviously too heavy for her, rounded the curve of the stairwell and started up the second half of the flight. Reynart pocketed the knife just as she lifted her gaze and saw him.

She gasped and dropped into a deep curtsey on the stairs, actually kneeling on one step while her basket rested on the step above. She bent her head and stared at the basket.

"I beg your forgiveness, my lord Prince. I did not see you."

"You're right. You didn't see me."

The girl lifted her head enough to peer through her bangs at him. "My lord Prince?"

"Go about your business, and tell no one that you saw us here. Katya, isn't it?"

"Yes, my lord Prince," she whispered. Her whole body trembled, rocking her basket and dislodging the top few pieces of kindling. With shaking hands, she gathered the fallen wood from the stairs, dropping the pieces back into her basket.

Angie couldn't understand the girl's obvious terror. Reynart had said nothing threatening. Then she realized that he didn't have to. He'd simply called the girl by name, implying that if anyone learned of Angie's presence, he'd hold her responsible, and would know how to find her. The thought of what he'd do then was obviously more than Katya could bear.

As if he realized he'd gone too far, Reynart's voice gentled. "There's no reason for you to fear, Katya. Simply do your work and say nothing. That's not so hard, is it?"

"No, my lord Prince." She shook her head violently, dislodging another two pieces of wood. As she scrambled to pick them up, she darted a second look upward through her bangs, this time at Angie.

Katya's eyes widened slightly before her head bent over her basket. Whoever she'd thought to see standing beside Reynart, it hadn't been Angie.

"Then be on your way," he ordered.

She bobbed her head, nearly knocking another piece of kindling to the stairs, and clenched her hands around the handle of her basket. Slowly, she rose to her feet, her head still bowed, and started up the stairs. Her body quivered with every step, as if she expected to be chastised at any moment for approaching the prince so closely.

She reached the head of the stairs, then sidled around him, never lifting her gaze from her white-knuckled grip on the basket.

"Oh, and Katya?" Reynart's casual question froze her in her tracks, making her tremble like a rabbit cornered by a cat.

"Yes, my lord Prince?" she whispered.

"Light the fire in the King's chambers first."

"Yes, my lord Prince."

He nodded, the gesture lost on the girl. "Then go."

"Yes, my lord Prince. Thank you."

She bolted for the open corridor, strewing bits of kindling in her wake. Reynart absently leaned down and retrieved them, as if he saw nothing unusual in a young servant being terrified out of her mind at the prospect of talking to him. Angie frowned. Maybe it wasn't unusual. But she was certain no one had ever been terrified of Lancelot.

As he straightened, she saw that his lips were moving ever so slightly. After a moment, she realized he was counting silently to himself.

"Thirty. Let's go. The guard is at the end of the hall. Stay close behind me and try to avoid being seen."

Angie gathered her skirts, so that she could run if she had to. Timing her steps with his, she followed Reynart like a shadow to the edge of the corridor, then peeked over his shoulder. The guard at the far end was just opening a door for the frightened chambermaid.

Reynart strode briskly down the corridor, forcing Angie into a trot to keep up with his longer stride. At the end of the hall, the guard turned to watch the chambermaid enter the room, briefly taking his eyes from the corridor.

Stopping at the first door on the left, Reynart whispered, "Open the door and get inside. Quickly!"

Angie grabbed the knob, twisted and shoved open the heavy door, ducking into the room beyond as soon as the opening was wide enough. She could see Reynart turning to face the door, even as he grabbed the knob and pulled it mostly shut.

She glanced quickly around the room, looking for possible hiding places in case the guard came to investigate. There were none. The room held a small table flanked by two plain wooden chairs, with another table and chair piled high with books and scrolls tucked beneath the window embrasure. A fireplace and a door shared the wall to her right, while shelves crowded with jars and boxes filled the wall on her left.

Guessing that the door led to Reynart's bedroom, she edged toward it. No doubt she could find some sliver of space to hide in, under the bed or inside the closet, if she needed to.

Her gaze was drawn back to the partially open door leading to the hallway. Reynart reached through the narrow opening, his hand flexing as if he was searching for something. Then he pushed the door wide open and entered the room, closing it behind him.

The brilliant smile he'd dazzled her with before flashed across his features again and he brushed his damp hair back, out of his eyes. His chest rose and fell with his deep breathing and she wondered if he'd been holding his breath the same way she had. Somehow, she doubted it. His smile was too self-confident, reminding her of one of the boys at school gloating when he'd put something over on a teacher. In fact, earlier she'd thought he was an adult, because of his attitude, but now that she really looked, he seemed very little older than she.

He tossed the kindling he held into the fireplace. "The guard noticed nothing. You're safe. For now, at least."

"How old are you?" she asked.

He blinked, then his face returned immediately to the shuttered and expressionless look he'd worn earlier. It was as if the very life drained out of it and she wanted to cry at the loss.

"That's right, you know nothing of my history. Where are you from that you are so ill-informed?"

She frowned, planting her fists on her hips and glaring at him. "I'm not ill-informed. Just because I've never heard of this place or you, Mr. High and Mighty, It's-All-About-Me Prince, doesn't mean that I don't know lots of other things. I'll have you know, I scored very well on my SATs."

For a moment, she worried that she'd gone too far. How could she have forgotten about the knife that jumped so easily to his hand?

Then he laughed.

Angie's breath escaped in a rush and she collapsed into one of the chairs beside the table. He shouldn't be allowed to do that. She'd thought he was gorgeous when he smiled but his laughter was like pure, crystallized joy. It was a drug to which she was instantly addicted. All she wanted was to make him happy, so he would laugh again.

But instead, he shook his head, and walked past her into the next room. She heard drawers sliding open and shut, then the whisper of leather on leather, followed by the sound of boots falling to the floor. Heat lightning flashed across her skin. He was getting undressed. The thought of him, so strong and powerful, being completely naked on the other side of that door, both thrilled and terrified her. By the time she'd composed herself, he'd returned.

Instead of the formfitting leather pants and tight boots, he wore loose gray pants that ended just below the knee, over gray hose that clung to his muscled calves. His burgundy embroidered velvet shoes glittered with seed pearls and chips of precious stones, as did the buckles at the knees of his pants. And he'd replaced the simple blue tunic with a tight gray undertunic and loose burgundy overtunic that was slashed and gathered to expose the layer underneath. He'd also added two silver and garnet rings, one on each hand, and a gleaming silver circlet that bound back his wavy black hair.

Angie stared at him in silence, before finally choking out, "I guess you really are a Prince."

"At the moment, anyway," he agreed, a completely confusing answer. "I must attend the King at dinner. It will likely be a number of hours until I return. You will have to stay here until then."

She nodded. "I can read a book or something."

A humorless smile ghosted across his face. "You are welcome to any of my books, although the analysis of the Conquest of Suddalyk makes for only slightly more interesting reading than the history of Tsieche trade contracts."

He was still in school, too! She grinned. "I'll manage."

"Touch nothing on the shelves. I will bring back food for you if I can."

"Thank you." For the first time, she realized he was putting himself at risk by hiding her. "Why are you helping me?"

His green eyes locked onto hers with a gaze of pure intensity that took her breath away. "I do not understand you. And I am unwilling for anything to happen to you until I learn who you are and what you are doing here."

"And once you learn that?"

"That depends on what I learn."

The total lack of emotion in his words sent a shiver of dread spiraling through her. She recalled the young chambermaid, terrified of displeasing the prince. What if he didn't like what he learned? Worse yet, what if he didn't believe Angie's story? She had no idea how she'd gotten here. If she couldn't explain herself to him, would he think she was holding out on him?

Her mind flashed on the stereotypical WWII movie, with the evil Nazi telling the bound hero, "Vee haf vays of making you talk."

But Reynart wasn't evil. He'd been nothing but kind and considerate, going out of his way to help her and protect her from this mage, Gervaise, who also seemed to be after her. As long as she was honest, she had nothing to fear from him.

She almost convinced herself that it was true.

He walked past her, bent down and picked up a thin cord from where it had fallen on the floor. Stretching it across the room, he fastened a loop at the end to a small hook on the back of the door. The hook was almost exactly where he'd pretended to feel around when he'd been getting the guard's attention while entering his room.

She followed the string to its other end. A crossbow hung suspended from the ceiling, cocked and ready, a wickedly barbed dart pointed at the door.

"You have a loaded crossbow aimed at the door?"

"I told you, no one comes in here without my permission. The crossbow is the first and most obvious deterrent."

Angie glanced nervously around the room, alert for any other traps. She couldn't see any. But then again, she hadn't noticed the crossbow until he'd called her attention to it by setting the trap.

"Is there anything I need to watch out for while you're gone? Any other traps I have to worry about setting off?"

Reynart considered, then shook his head. "Don't touch the shelves and you'll be fine."

Then he slipped out the door, leaving her alone in the room.

She breathed deeply, working to convince herself that it was really safe to move around the room. Slowly, she inched her way across the stone floor to the desk and picked up one of the books.

The language it was printed in was incomprehensible gobbledygook. She opened all of the books and unrolled the scrolls, searching for anything recognizable, but they were all covered in the same unreadable flowing script. Whatever magic enabled her to understand Reynart as if he was speaking English apparently didn't extend to the written word.

She stared at the pile of papers on the desk in disgust. "Great. Now what am I supposed to do for the next few hours?"

Slowly, a smile spread across her face. Reynart had said to leave the shelves alone. He hadn't said anything about drawers or closets. It was time to learn a little more about her Prince, in the time honored way. She was going to snoop through his things.

After glancing once more around the sitting room, she turned and entered his bedroom.

* * * * *

"What do you think of that plan?" The King turned away from General Cort, who sat between him and the Queen on his right, to where Reynart sat on his left. It was the fourth night in a row that Reynart had been given the place of honor over Alaric and his brother was furious that he was too far away to hear the General's low comments. In retaliation, he'd turned and held a whispered conversation with the mage Gervaise, to his left, pointedly excluding Reynart.

Alaric's whispers stilled as he dropped the pretense to listen to Reynart's response.

"Lord General Cort is correct that the uprisings in Sudern must be put down swiftly. And his proposed plan would break the rebel's spirits. But I question using the same tactics we used last year. If they were not sufficiently cowed by their defeat last year to remain subservient, why does he think they will not find new leaders and rise up again next year?"

"He plans to execute not just the leaders, but their families as well. Men who are not afraid to die will hesitate before risking their families." The King tried to keep his voice impassive but his scorn at this weak sentimentality bled through.

That was enough of a clue that Reynart was certain of the correct answer. "They will simply find leaders who have no families. Unmarried sons of last year's rebels, no doubt, with a personal need for vengeance fueling their hate."

"What would you suggest?"

This was a trickier answer. Was the King asking because he truly wanted to know what Reynart thought? Or was he testing his son, matching Reynart's response against what he'd already determined to be the correct course of action?

Hoping he'd chosen correctly, and because he couldn't imagine what other course of action the King could have decided upon, Reynart offered his true opinion.

"Give them what they want."

"What?" the King thundered. The hall fell silent as all eyes turned to the high table.

"Your Majesty, the rebels claim the right of self-determination and demand a return to self-sovereignty. Obviously, you will not relinquish the province and they are fools to even suggest it." Reynart took a deep breath as the flush faded from the King's face. That was too close.

The other diners resumed their conversations, filling the hall with a soft, if somewhat strained, murmur of sound.

"Then what do you suggest?" the King asked, his clipped tones making it quite clear that Reynart had better not suggest giving up any of his power.

"What you have done in the past, Your Majesty. When you conquered the province of Kittern, you secured the rebellious natives by marrying your baron to one of the local nobility."

The King frowned. "Kittern was a special case."

"But the same principle would apply. Let the rebels know that you feel your current baron does not understand them well enough to rule. The man should be removed from his position anyway, for allowing two uprisings in two years. Appoint a new baron, an unmarried baron, and have him choose a bride from among the conquered nobility. But for the Pair's sake, have him treat her well. So long as the people feel they may approach her with their complaints and she will be heard by her husband, they will use that route, rather than armed warfare."

The King sipped his goblet of wine as he considered, then nodded sharply. A servant hurried forward to refill the goblet as soon as it was once more resting on the table.

"Who would you suggest as the new baron?"

Reynart lowered his eyes, bowing his head to his father. "I would not presume to suggest someone to you, Your Majesty. You know far better than I who among your nobles could best be trusted with an appointment such as this."

Alaric choked off a snort behind him, no doubt certain that Reynart could easily name two or three men who would be perfect for the post. His ability to remember the names, careers, alliances and allegiances of the entire court and officers of the army had been a running joke between them for years, before Alaric became determined to see all of Reynart's skills and abilities as direct slights and attempts to cement his position as the King's heir. Maybe Alaric's amusement was a sign that things were returning to how they had been.

Alaric would have been right. Reynart knew of three people who would be well suited for the position, and one who would be perfect. The noble hailed from a province with similar climate and agriculture, and due to an injury, was the only one among the King's most trusted nobles who had not fought in this year's battles. But having narrowly evaded one killing blow already tonight, Reynart saw no reason to start another duel. He would concede this battle to his father.

The King grunted and turned to General Cort. "Who would you recommend as the new baron and as the local noblewoman he should take for his wife?"

The King's voice was louder this time, easily heard by the servants and the nobles at the front of the tables below them. The King was going to take Reynart's advice. By morning, messengers would already be riding for the disputed province, relaying the rumor that the King was thinking of raising one of their own to be baroness.

"Well handled, brother," Alaric said softly. "I feared for your safety—and your sanity—when you offered to give the rebels what they wanted. Had I offered such a suggestion, I would have been branded a coward, to try and solve a conflict without bloodshed."

Reynart shook his head, wishing he could take the bitterness from his younger brother's eyes. "Last year was your first battle. When you acquit yourself well this year, all will see that you made an error of inexperience last year, not of cowardice."

"And will you be riding with me again, to fix my errors with another spectacular charge against the enemy?"

"Alaric, we have discussed this. Repeatedly. A man's life was in danger."

"You could have told me you'd seen him survive having his horse cut out from under him. You didn't need to stage the heroic rescue attempt yourself."

"I was closer to him than to you. And my troops were already positioned for another charge."

"Mother said—" Alaric bit off his words but it was too late. Reynart felt the familiar stiffening of his facial features as he thought of the woman whose sole purpose in life was to discredit him in favor of her son.

"The Queen, your mother, knows nothing of military tactics or strategy. You would be well advised to remember that."

Chapter Three

After the interminable dinner, during which Reynart's thoughts were much occupied with the mysterious woman he'd left in his rooms, the King rose and they were finally free to leave. General Cort, his wife and the mage Gervaise left the strained atmosphere of the high table immediately, leaving only the three remaining members of the royal family. Reynart beckoned to one of the serving children and requested a selection of meat and cheese from the kitchen that he could take back to his chambers.

"His Majesty's displeasure made you lose your appetite?" Alaric asked.

Reynart just smiled. He'd long since learned never to explain himself to servants and to his family only when necessary.

The Queen paused as she passed them. "I heard your…unusual solution to the uprisings. Are you hoping the King will name you to the barony?"

Only long practice kept him from stiffening beneath her insult. He was a prince of Nord D'Rae, currently next in line for the throne. The rank of baron was far beneath him.

But he knew better than to respond with any words she could twist and take to the King. "His Majesty will, I am sure, choose wisely."

"Then he will not choose you. Such a position calls for someone of unquestioned loyalty and the highest breeding. It would be an insult to the conquered people to marry off their chosen noblewoman to a maid's bastard."

Behind him, Alaric caught his breath.

"As I said, I am certain the King will choose wisely."

The Queen sniffed, then swept through the door in a rustle of velvet and jewel-encrusted silk. Alaric hesitated a moment longer, then asked, "*Are* you thinking of asking for the position?"

Something in his brother's voice made Reynart turn and study him before answering. His eyes held the same wary blend of fear and regret that Reynart recognized from countless childhood escapades, when Alaric's quick temper had led him to take an action whose wisdom he later questioned. Was he now regretting having baited Reynart during dinner?

"I will, of course, do as His Majesty bids. But I will not seek service through marriage." He offered a brotherly smile, hoping to recapture some of the camaraderie that had existed between them before this summer's disastrous campaign. "If I am to return to that province, I would far rather return with a captaincy than a barony."

Alaric turned away. "The boy has returned with your foodstuffs. Pleasant dining, brother."

Reynart released his breath on a sigh as his brother left the room, back stiff and eyes staring straight ahead. Taking the gathered cloth from the boy, he followed his brother back to the private wing of the castle without trying to catch up to him or speak to him.

Alaric refused to believe that Reynart had not purposely tried to discredit him. Perhaps because Alaric had spent so many years admiring his older brother's prowess with a sword, he had been reckless and too eager to prove himself when finally given the chance. He had overextended his forces and the enemy had broken their line. He'd had no choice but to retreat and regroup. A foolish mistake, but understandable on his first campaign.

Abandoning his fallen lieutenant, on the other hand, had been unforgivable, especially since Reynart's quick actions had been able to save the man. It did not matter that Alaric had only seen the horse go down in a cluster of fighting and had been unable to see the lieutenant kick free of the stirrups before his horse fell and continue the fight on foot. The King had declared Alaric a coward.

That night, when the King summoned Reynart to his tent to tell him that Alaric's troops were to be added to Reynart's command, Reynart had pled Alaric's case. He'd begged the King to give Alaric a second chance, earning a vicious cut from the King's riding crop across his face for his troubles. Alaric, no doubt under his mother's persuasion, believed the King had asked Reynart for his interpretation of what had occurred and Reynart had elaborated upon Alaric's mistake while highlighting his own actions, until he persuaded the King to give him his brother's command.

A foolish dispute. If the meddling Queen would just stay out of it and the two brothers dared to openly ask the King why he had acted as he did, all could be resolved. But the Heavenly Pair would descend and walk among their people before that ever happened.

Reynart disabled the crossbow trap on his door and entered his room, surprised to find it dark. He stepped to the side so that he would not be silhouetted in the doorway, scanning for another presence in the room. Why had Anjeli not lit the fire, or at least a candle?

He closed the door softly, letting his eyes adjust to the darkened room. When he could see that it was empty, he walked cautiously forward, dropping the food onto the table as he passed. The door to his bedroom was open and no light shone through the doorway.

Staying close to the wall and alert for a possible attack, he listened carefully, but heard no sound from the other side. Slowly, he peered around the door frame.

Anjeli lay on his bed, asleep. Her braids had come undone, falling about her head and across her face in disarray, and her skirt had hitched up to expose one leg from her knee down.

Reynart's breath caught, his loins tightening at the sight. Her leg was straight and well-muscled, with a delicate ankle and toes that glittered with some mysterious anointment of female beauty. Despite his better instincts, he found himself drawn to her side, standing at the foot of the bed and reaching out to stroke a fingertip over the soft sole of her foot.

Her foot twitched in response, like a horse kicking to dislodge a fly, and her skirt fell further askew, revealing a glimpse of her other ankle. He felt himself hardening, his spear at the ready for the battle frenzy ahead. It would be the simplest of movements to grasp her slender calf, tug her onto her back and spread her legs wide. His palms itched to feel her smooth skin beneath his hands as he caressed her legs, pushing her heavy skirt up and out of the way until his way was clear. Even though it had been months since he'd last had a woman, he wouldn't rush. He'd take the time to ensure she was well pleased, too.

His spear trembled with eagerness but, other than that, Reynart did not move. All he had to do was reach out and turn her. Yet his hands remained loosely fisted at his sides.

He did not want to leap into the fray. Not when Anjeli rested on his bed as if she had every right to be there, trusting that she would be safe. Something painful twisted in his chest, and he struggled for breath, blinking his suddenly blurry eyes into focus. Whatever else was true about her, and she had much yet to explain, he had no doubt that, where men and women were concerned, she was an innocent.

He should light a fire in the sitting room, wrap himself in his cloak and sleep on the floor. One night would not bother him. He had plenty of practice sleeping before hearths and in piles of straw.

Instead, he reached out and once again stroked her foot. Slowly, he teased her skirt higher, exposing her other leg, then a glimpse of her thigh. His spear was hard as an oaken staff and pressing forward for battle. But he feared any battle would be over before he had fairly engaged, as he could barely breathe and his spear trembled like a first-time campaigner's.

Anjeli muttered softly in her sleep and swatted vaguely at her legs with one sleep-loosened arm before burrowing her face deeper into the pillow. Her skirt rode higher, showing both thighs and a hint of shadow between them, before being knocked down to cover both legs to her knees by her returning arm. Reynart groaned.

He turned away and forced himself to carefully remove his court clothing, returning it to the armoire. Soon he was naked except for his vambraces. Normally, he would wear those to bed, hating to be without a weapon instantly at hand. But a throwing dagger was not the weapon he wanted to be using tonight.

He unlaced both vambraces, placing one in the armoire and taking the other to slide beneath his pillow where he could hold it while he slept.

Standing beside the bed, watching Anjeli's deep and even breathing, he debated his next course of action. What eventually decided him was that she trusted him enough to fall asleep unprotected in his bed. He could not betray that trust, no matter how enticing a picture she made.

He sighed, then regretfully lifted the down comforter and slid between the sheets. The down bedtop beneath him cradled his body, the delicate feathers shifting and sliding like a ghostly lover's caress, and he groaned again at the price of his foolishness.

Pushing the comforter nearly to his waist, he reached out and wrapped his arm lightly around Anjeli's body. She muttered again in her sleep and snuggled closer to the heat of his body.

He pulled her closer, turning her and fitting her hips to his. His spear pushed the intervening feathers of the comforter away to the sides, until he could feel the soft cleft of her backside through the now featherless covering. Slowly, he gathered the fabric of her skirt, lifting it away until her sweet flesh was exposed. He pulled her tighter still, his spear nestling in the valley he revealed, only the satin fabric of the comforter between them.

A low groan escaped his lips. She was so sweet. If he slid his hand beneath her skirt to tease between her legs, would she arch and rub herself against him? Would her softly uttered dream words be replaced by soft cries of building passion?

Cursing himself for being seven kinds of fool, he twitched her skirt over her legs, keeping them warm. He cupped one hand around a breast, stroking the exposed upper surface lightly with his thumb, and pressed his chest flush against her back, his head resting on her pillow, with her head tucked beneath his chin.

His remaining hand slipped under his pillow and clasped the hilt of a throwing knife.

* * * * *

Angie drifted slowly toward wakefulness, dimly aware that she had been warm and now was cold. There was warmth at her back and she reached blindly behind her, fumbling for the soft comforter, which she pulled back over herself.

It was just as quickly pulled off.

"Pull up the other side, if you're cold. This side's mine," a sleepy voice muttered.

A *man's* voice.

Angie froze, a flood of adrenaline bringing her instantly awake. She was lying on top of a bed, a man's warm body pressed close behind her, his arm draped loosely across her.

Reynart.

It hadn't been a dream.

She pushed his arm away and rolled to the other side of the bed, then turned back, fearful of what she might see. He lay on his side, mostly covered by the disputed comforter, except for the bare arm that he'd been holding her with.

He opened his eyes and looked at her. "At least you didn't wake up screaming."

"What are you doing here?"

"I was sleeping." He glanced at the dim gray outline of the embrasure in the wall. "Something I had hoped to continue doing for a few more candlemarks."

He wanted her to sleep next to him? In the same bed? He wasn't wearing a shirt! Her breath caught in her chest and she studiously avoided looking at the contours of his body under the comforter, staring at his face. "Are you wearing any clothing?"

"It is not cold enough to need a night shirt." That deadly grin burst across his features again, his green eyes twinkling in the dim morning light. "It is cold enough, however, to want a coverlet."

Her cheeks burned. "I'm sorry."

His expression turned serious. "I did not wish to presume when I found you asleep, so I left you on top of the coverlet. But you will stay warmer if you join me beneath it."

"You're just trying to make sure I don't steal all the covers." She forced a lighthearted tone, not entirely certain of what he was asking and, if he was asking what she thought he was asking, not entirely certain of what her answer would be.

"That, too," he agreed.

"Too?"

He lowered his gaze to the comforter, absently smoothing it with his hand. "You are very pleasant to hold."

A warm glow of pleasure rushed through her body, making her skin tingle. He liked holding her. So maybe there was something more between them than simple chivalry and curiosity.

"Okay," she whispered, before she could lose her nerve.

His answering smile heated her body down to her toes. He sat up, the comforter falling to his waist, exposing his well-muscled chest.

Angie's eyes widened. At least a dozen thin white lines scored his chest, at all different angles and lengths, along with a handful of patches where the skin was pink and shiny. Her throat tightened.

"What happened?" she whispered.

It was the wrong question to ask. She saw the impassive expression close down his features again, his eyes going cold and stony, his jaw thrusting ever so slightly forward. "Come here and turn around. You need to remove the outer layer of your gown or you will overheat."

Considering he was offering to undress her, it was the most unromantic suggestion she'd ever heard. Had he made the offer a moment ago, with his teasing grin, she'd have eagerly stood before him, trembling, as his strong hands skimmed over her body, lifting away the heavy wool and velvet dress, leaving her clad only in the thin chemise. But not now. Not when he stared at her out of cold eyes that terrified her with their complete lack of humanity.

He snorted. "Then you can sleep atop the coverlet again."

Pulling up the comforter, this time over his arm, he turned onto his side again and closed his eyes. His body language said quite clearly that he neither wanted nor needed her beside him. The small flower of hope that had begun blossoming within her withered at the sight.

She swallowed, struggling against a lump in her throat that threatened to choke her. He didn't really like her. At all. So what if he was the most gorgeous man she'd ever seen? Even with all those scars. They only increased his air of danger, mute testament of…

She blinked. She had no idea what the scars were mute testament of. Some bizarre training regimen? Religious ritual? Past battles? Tragic accident? He'd refused to answer her question, then distracted her by turning away.

The tiny bud of hope revived, bursting into full flower.

She crawled across the comforter and turned her back to him. "I tried to untie it earlier, when I lay down, but I couldn't figure out how the laces worked."

There was a moment of silence from the man behind her, then he sat up and began unlacing her gown. She breathed deeply, welcoming the freedom from the tight cage of the gown's bodice.

"All done," he said softly.

"Thank you." She climbed off the bed. Facing away from him, she slowly lifted the gown up and over her head, leaving only the silky chemise clinging to her skin. Behind her, she heard Reynart catch his breath.

Carefully, she folded the gown and stowed it in his armoire. She clutched the handle, staring at the closed door of the closet, while she listened to his soft breathing. She had to turn around eventually. She had to face him.

One finger at a time, she released the solid security of the handle. Then she turned around.

If he said anything, she was certain she'd lose her nerve. She was planning on sharing a bed with a naked man!

She ran her damp palms down her thighs, smoothing the soft fabric of her chemise. It was like wearing a nightgown. At least she wouldn't be naked with him.

Flames licked her cheeks at the mental image that arose of the two of them, naked and making out, his strong hands stroking her skin while he kissed her senseless. A strangled noise of protest escaped her throat. She couldn't do this. She couldn't.

Reynart pushed aside the comforter, revealing a sheet across his legs. Angie's eyes widened, then she chuckled. Of course. They would be sharing the heat of the comforter, but still separated by a sheet.

She breathed easier and walked over to the bed. Yet, she was aware of a deep disappointment. She'd been frightened of sharing his bed but, at the same time, she'd anticipated how it would feel to have his warm, strong body curled protectively around hers, holding her tight through the rest of the night.

Looking up from his sheet-draped legs, she met his darkened gaze. He glanced down the length of her chemise, lingering in the places where the thin fabric clung to her hips and fluttered about her calves. She shivered under his candid regard.

When his gaze returned to her eyes, his scarred chest rose and fell with his deep breaths and admiration shone in the depths of his emerald eyes. One black eyebrow lifted slightly in silent question, and he placed his hand lightly on the sheet, gathering it into his fist.

Angie moistened her parched lips, hypnotized by the desire in his eyes. No one had ever looked at her like that before. She couldn't breathe, her blood pounding in her ears as her skin flushed first hot then icy cold.

She nodded. Reynart pushed the sheet aside as well, then held out his hand. Slowly, moving as if in a dream, she reached out and clasped his hand. His fingers closed about hers, drawing her onto the bed, then pulling her down beside him.

He nudged her onto her side, then curled up behind her. She held her breath as he covered them, then wrapped his arm around her, pulling her tight against him.

His hip dug into her backside and she wriggled, trying to find a more comfortable position. He hissed, his arm tightening so sharply he forced the air from her lungs.

"You don't want to do that, Anjeli," he whispered. "Unless you intend to leave this bed no longer a maid."

She froze. That wasn't his hip digging into her. It was his…his… She swallowed and inhaled short, shallow breaths that pressed her ribs against the iron band of his arm.

"Uh, no," she said, mentally berating herself for sounding like the world's biggest idiot. But how could he expect her to think when he was lying behind her naked, with his you-know-what poking her in the backside?

He chuckled softly, his breath stirring her hair, and softened his iron grip. "No, you don't want to do that? Or no, you don't want to leave this bed a maid?"

But he didn't seem to expect an answer, shifting against her so that his hot length was nestled between her ass cheeks, no longer poking her, but still hard and strong, focusing her awareness on the unimagined maleness of him.

"Relax," he murmured, snuggling closer, so that he enfolded her like a living blanket. Her back was cradled by his muscled chest, her thighs rested against his bent legs and her head nestled in the hollow between his shoulder and jaw. The weight of his arm rested possessively around her ribs.

She closed her eyes and breathed deeply, savoring the sensation of being cherished and cared for. Tentatively, she rested her hand on his arm. When he didn't protest, she ran her fingertips lightly over his skin, tracing the contours of his bones and muscles.

His deep sigh of pleasure ruffled her hair. Shifting his arm slightly, he brushed her breast lightly with his fingertips. She gasped at the unexpected touch, instinctively tensing. He waited for her breathing to steady before he stroked her again.

She didn't tense, this time. There was nothing threatening in his touch. Only a soft, gentle whisper of his fingertips against her chemise-covered skin.

Relaxing into his sleepy caress, she petted and stroked his muscled arm and dreamed of a vague future when the liquid heat within her would turn to passion and love.

* * * * *

Angie sighed, warm and content. The bed rocked softly beneath her, rising and falling like a boat bobbing on the merest hint of waves. A gentle hand stroked from the nape of her neck, down her back, to cup and caress her backside, before rising to trail another soft caress up to her neck.

She inhaled deeply, filling her lungs with Reynart's subtle, spicy scent. She was sprawled across him like a second comforter but he didn't seem to mind.

"Good morning," she mumbled.

"That it is."

His hand continued to glide up and down her back with long, firm strokes that pressed her body against his. She leaned on her forearms, lifting herself up to look at his face.

He grunted and tugged her leg all the way across him, so that she straddled his waist. Having moved his hand, he kept it there, alternating between caressing her backside and cupping it to pull her tighter against him.

The hot ridge of his hard-on pressed between her open legs, teasing her with a light touch that made her ache for something more. Her eyes widened, a soft exclamation whispering between her lips as she realized what exactly she longed for.

Staring into his deep green eyes, she watched him watching her. He cupped her backside again, drawing her against his cock, but this time he lifted his hips slightly as he did so, pressing up against her.

"Oh," she breathed.

He did it again.

"Reynart?" she whispered. "Would you…kiss me?"

"Gladly."

He rolled them so that she was pinned beneath him. He looked down at her flushed and wide-eyed face, searching for some answer in her eyes. Whatever he saw must have been the right response, because he lowered his head and claimed her lips with his.

The kiss was everything that Angie had dreamed. His lips were warm and firm, brushing back and forth across hers with a teasing caress before he covered her mouth with his. The pressure of his mouth on hers gradually built, until her lips parted with a sigh.

He continued to strengthen the kiss, increasing the pressure of his mouth on hers and gradually forcing her mouth open. Then his tongue brushed gently across her lower lip. He drew her lower lip into his mouth, sucking on it and feathering it with soft caresses from his tongue.

She groaned, the gentle tugging only increasing the ache between her legs.

Reynart lifted his head, breaking the kiss and smiling down upon her. "It's all right for you to kiss me in return, you know."

Her cheeks burned at his teasing admonishment. He must think she was a complete idiot!

Then she saw the warmth in his eyes and the gentleness of his smile. No, he knew this was her first real kiss. He didn't mind if she didn't know quite what she was doing.

Raising both hands, she buried her fingers in his hair, then drew his head back down, meeting his mouth with her own. This time she pulled his lip into her mouth, suckling it and stroking it with her tongue.

He groaned, then claimed her mouth for his own, thrusting his tongue inside, stroking and caressing. They suckled and stroked, nipped and nibbled, until they were both breathless. Angie writhed beneath him, moaning and trembling with longing.

Then he shifted his hips, pressing the hot length of his erection between her legs. She arched upward, whimpering with need. He moved, sliding his manhood back and forth as he slipped his tongue in and out of her mouth.

Her hands smoothed down the slick planes of his back to grab his backside, urging him to move harder and faster against her.

He lifted his lips from hers, shifting to press hot, openmouthed kisses down her jaw and on the pulsing vein in her neck. She moaned, her head thrashing from side to side, as the deep need continued building inside her. His hips flexed, grinding his erection against the tender flesh between her legs, again and again, until she thought she'd go insane if he didn't do something to satisfy the throbbing ache.

His tempo changed, rocking faster and faster against her. She couldn't catch her breath, couldn't think, couldn't do anything but lift her hips again and again in time to his movements, aching and reaching for an end to the need that consumed her.

Then a wave of heat and pleasure burst over her, flooding her and making her cry out in surprise. Reynart continued rocking against her, faster and faster, his breath hoarse and ragged with effort. Then he rolled off of her, eyes squeezed tightly shut as he cried out.

Her first thought was that she'd done something wrong. But he soothed that fear by pulling her arm around him, so that she now cradled him. He brushed a brief kiss across her knuckles, then let her hand fall so that her arm draped across his naked body. His stomach was covered with hot, sticky wetness.

He chuckled at her sound of dismay, clamping hold of her arm and refusing to let her escape. "I didn't want to ruin your garment."

Flames burned in her face again as she realized what was under her hand. But at least she knew she hadn't done anything wrong.

He wrapped her body more tightly around his and, as his breathing returned to normal, said softly, "Next time, take off the chemise."

Chapter Four

Reynart relaxed into the warmth of the woman behind him as his heart and breathing slowed. That had been far more than a simple kiss. Yet just the whisper of Anjeli's breath across his shoulder and the trembling touch of her hand against his stomach was enough to raise his spear, readying for a second charge. An ineffectual charge as yet but, if she continued rubbing against him as she was doing, that would soon change.

"Reynart?" she asked softly. "Was that…sex?"

He closed his eyes, silently calling down the Heavenly Pair's harshest judgment upon members of the nobility who thought to keep their daughters available for profitable marriage alliances by keeping them ignorant. Knowledge was always preferable to ignorance.

"No. You are still a maiden."

"Oh." She was silent for several minutes, thinking about it. Then, tentatively, she asked, "But it was very much like sex, wasn't it?"

"Yes. Very much."

He sighed, realizing he was going to have to have this conversation with her, no matter how awkward it was. Twining his fingers with hers, he brought her hand down to rest on the haft of his spear. She gasped softly but her fingers closed around him, feeling the strength of him.

"That is my spear," he told her.

"It felt…harder earlier. And hotter."

"Yes, that's what happens when a man is with a woman he finds pleasing." As it was happening now, with her hand wrapped around him. He took a deep breath and continued his explanation. "While holding or touching a man's spear is enjoyable for the man or having him rub it back and forth against a woman's barbican may be enjoyable for them both, it is only when she raises the portcullis and allows him entry into the keep that it is sex."

She remained quiet for another long minute, her fingers idly stroking up and down his haft, driving him half insane with her feather soft caresses. "What's a barbican?"

"Oh, for the Pair's sake," he groaned. Rolling over, he grabbed the hem of her chemise and yanked it up to her breasts. He reached between her legs, his fingers slipping through the wet heat of her earlier pleasure, until he found the outbuilding of her womanly castle. Rubbing the swollen flesh, he declared, "This is a barbican."

She moaned, arching herself against his hand.

He continued to fondle her, her soft gasps and low groans filling him with masculine pleasure that he was the one who could bring her to such a state. Shifting his hand further back, he found her outer gates already wide open and the inner pair well on their way. He circled his finger around the hot, wet flesh, pressing lightly.

"This is your portcullis," he whispered.

Anjeli turned onto her back, her legs spread wide in invitation. He knelt between her legs, his fingers teasing the opening wider while she moaned and bucked beneath his hand, urging his fingers to slip inside. At last, when she had opened her portcullis enough to grant two fingers entry and nearly wide enough for three, he pressed further inside. Almost immediately, he found the thin wall that half filled the opening beyond.

"Amin-ra take it," he cursed softly. He wasn't about to hurt her when she was just learning about her body. Carefully, he slipped one finger past the wall. Stroking his finger in and out, over her portcullis, he rubbed her barbican with his thumb.

Her breath came faster and faster, in short, hitched gasps between soft cries. She trembled uncontrollably, her hips bouncing, as she begged for her release. Her clawing fingers gathered up a handful of coverlet, clenching the down tightly in her fist. She arched her back and cried out, before collapsing limply onto the bed, her hand falling open to release the mangled bedclothes.

Reynart continued stroking her gently, soothing her but keeping her wide open, just in case. Her eyelids fluttered open and she smiled drowsily up at him.

"You can storm my castle anytime."

He chuckled. He was pleased that she had enjoyed her lesson, and only hoped she would find the next one to her liking as well.

"That was only my hand. To truly storm your castle, I would need to use my spear."

"Mmm, okay."

She had no idea what she was agreeing to. He tried to explain. "There is a door, just inside the portcullis. The first time, it must be forced open."

"Raise the portcullis, force the door. Got it."

He bit his lip. "No. I mean forced."

Something about his tone finally penetrated her haze of pleasure and she struggled up to her elbows to look at him. She paled, and swallowed heavily. "How much force?"

"The door must be ripped from its hinges."

She winced, instinctively trying to close her legs although, since he was kneeling between them, she couldn't. He felt her muscles tensing around his fingers.

"It will hurt," he admitted. "I will not lie to you and say it will not. But I am told the pain passes quickly. And then you can feel the pleasure of having a man's spear thrust deeply inside you."

"I don't want a man's spear inside me."

Reynart's fingers stilled. That was her choice.

"I want *your* spear inside me."

A sweet warmth, like the Heavenly Pair's holy flame, spread out from his heart to encompass his entire body. He had never been offered such a precious gift, to be a woman's first and only man. Indeed, like all men of the nobility, he sought women who'd had multiple liaisons, so that he would never find himself forced into a politically inadvantageous marriage by an unwanted pregnancy.

He was intimately familiar with that particular area of the law, since his unusual status depended upon it. So long as his father admitted Reynart was his son, he and Reynart's mother were considered married in the eyes of the Heavenly Pair, since they had created a child together. That made Reynart the eldest non-mage child and, thus, heir to the throne. However, since there had been no wedding ceremony, whenever the King changed his mind and declared that he'd been mistaken, Reynart became instead the unwanted bastard child of a dead maid and was thrown out to fend for himself. He suspected in other cases, a declaration of parentage one way or the other was considered binding but, as with so many other things, that stipulation did not apply to the King.

Briefly, he considered that Anjeli might have been sent to try and trap him into just such an alliance. But even if she was a far better actress than the most skilled traveling player, the logistics of knowing he would be in that hallway at that time to find her, as well as there being virtually no benefit to such a marriage, convinced him that it was a groundless fear.

She still might become pregnant. That was a risk he was willing to take, if it meant he would be the one to show her the heights of pleasure a man and a woman could share.

He hesitated. She'd known so little. What if she had never been told this, as well?

"You realize, once my spear enters your keep, it is possible you could have a child?"

The delicate skin of her cheeks paled again. Amin-ra take both her parents for stupid fools!

"I hadn't thought that far..." She moistened her lips and gazed up at him. "Is it likely?"

"Not likely, no. I've already spent my seed once and there will be little enough for a second charge."

"Then do it."

Carefully, he positioned the head of his spear in the opening beneath her portcullis. She tensed as she felt him pressing against her. That was no good. It would hurt her more if she was tense.

He splayed his hands over her hips, soothing and caressing her but, at the same time, making certain she would not move.

"I told you, the next time you needed to remove your chemise," he reminded her.

As he'd hoped, she chuckled and turned her attention to untangling the garment currently wrapped around her chest, then lifting it over her head. He waited until she had almost removed it, her thoughts focused completely on her chemise. Then he tightened his grip on her hips and thrust through her barrier.

She cried out and tried to pull away from him. He held firm, covering her body with his, dusting her lips and cheeks with soft kisses.

"You're right. That hurt."

He heard the tremor in her voice as she fought to distance herself from her natural reaction. Using her words to reach out to him when her body would not.

Agony knifed through him, that he had hurt her, when all he wanted was to please her. Bracing his weight on one arm, he brushed her hair out of her eyes with a hand held stiff to keep it from trembling and searched the clear blue depths of her eyes.

"But was I also correct that the pain passes?"

She blinked, a thoughtful expression on her face, then her eyes widened. The muscles of her keep tightened around his spear, loosening then tightening again. He struggled to remember how to breathe.

"That's you?"

"That's me."

"You're right. This does feel wonderful."

He smiled and brushed another kiss across her lips. "This is only the beginning."

Then he began to move. Slowly, drawing his spear out until only the head remained beyond her portcullis, he hovered in her gateway, then changed directions and pressed deep within. She sighed and moaned with each slow stroke and huskily whispered, "Again."

Their rhythm built gradually, until neither had the breath or wit for speech; harsh gasps and cries were enough to convey what touches pleased them. Even as he plunged his spear into her over and over again, Reynart found it wasn't enough to storm her castle. He needed to possess her completely.

He covered her face, her throat, her ears and her hair with a flurry of kisses, while his hands roamed over her body, stroking her sides and kneading her breasts. She moaned and writhed, turning into his touch like a plant seeking the sun. Her hands clenched his shoulders, seeking his strength.

He gasped, recognizing the final buildup. He thrust faster and faster, straining to reach just a little farther, until he knew he'd gone as deeply as he could go. He arched upward, crushing his hips against hers, his arms trembling with his weight. Then he hurled his spear, flooding her keep with his seed.

Beneath him, Anjeli continued to whimper and moan, bucking her hips. He reached between their bodies, past his spent spear, and found her swollen barbican. He teased and squeezed it, rubbing his thumb back and forth as her cries rose higher and higher in pitch, until she gave one last cry, shuddered and fell still.

A sudden sense of incredible power coursed through him. Partly, it was the familiar masculine triumph of having brought her to climax. But a lover's pleasure had never affected him so deeply before. No, this maiden had invited him into her body not for money, or political favor or even just because she enjoyed lying with men. She had let down her keep's defenses because she wanted him, and only him, inside her.

He couldn't describe the feeling that welled up inside him. He only knew that she was his and he would kill anyone that tried to take her from him.

He nudged her limp body onto her side, then curled up behind her and drew the covers over them both. She sighed softly and pulled his arm tighter around her.

"Well?" he whispered, nibbling gently on her earlobe because it was there and he could.

She nodded her head a fraction and murmured, "Yes."

Reynart reached up and gently tweaked her nose. "Wake up, sleepyhead. My question called for more than a yes or no."

"Doesn't matter. I saved time and answered all of your questions. Did I like it? Were you right? Would I do it again? Yes."

He sighed deeply, at peace with the world, and wrapped his arm around her again, holding this precious woman close. "Yes," he agreed.

* * * * *

Angie woke to the sound of distant bells, followed almost immediately by Reynart hugging her close beneath the toasty comforter and nuzzling her neck with sleepy kisses. She smiled, remembering what they had shared in the middle of the night, but also the way he'd held her through the night like his own personal teddy bear.

Twice during the night, ringing bells had awakened her. Each time, his arms had tightened around her, as if he sensed her distress. Each time, she had been comforted by his concern and drifted back to sleep secure in his embrace.

"Greetings of the morning to you," he whispered, stroking her back and feathering his fingers through the remains of her braids.

"Good morning. You made an excellent pillow."

He chuckled softly but seemed in no hurry to push her off so that he could get up.

"Thank you, milady. And you made an excellent coverlet. Never before have I stayed so warm through the night."

She'd thrown her leg across his hips at some point during the night and now his spear, as he called it, pressed upward against her thigh, leaving her in no doubt about the source of his heat.

"You want to make love again?"

"Gladly would I storm your castle, milady. Even now, my battering ram stands at the ready." He exhaled loudly. "But from all I have heard, you will want no one passing beneath your portcullis for two or three days."

That funny itch was back again, deep inside her. But now she knew what it was. Her body hungered for his, to feel him bursting inside her.

She shifted, trying to center herself on top of him, so that his cock would be pressing on the part of her that ached for his possession instead of against her thigh. The movement stretched muscles she hadn't even known she'd had until last night and she winced.

Instantly, Reynart rolled her onto her back, lying on his side next to her. He stroked his fingers lightly over her stomach, then cupped and caressed one of her breasts.

She moaned softly, arching into his touch.

"You would not be pleased if I were to take you now and I want nothing so much as to please you." He leaned over her and kissed her lips, his mouth gentle on hers. The moment stretched, the touch of his kiss and the soft caress of his hand sweeping her thoughts away to a place where only feelings existed.

Too soon, he lifted his head and moved his hand to the safer region of her hip.

"Alas, I fear I am doomed to disappoint you in this as well."

His voice was light but, when she opened her eyes, his dark gaze pled mutely for her forgiveness. She reached up to cup his cheek and he closed his eyes, pressing his cheek into her hand.

Her chest felt suddenly filled with shards of glass, so that even breathing was an excruciating pain. How could she have been so blind? He'd given her plenty of clues. The way he'd stared at her hand when she first took his fingers in hers, the gentle reverence with which he touched her, his need to hold her close, even while fast asleep.

She pictured her mother's favorite self-help guru, the jovial Leo Buscaglia, who encouraged people to love one another, even hugging the strangers in the audience at his talks. When was the last time anyone had hugged

Reynart? When was the last time he'd been touched with gentleness and love? He was clearly starving for affection.

Immediately on the heels of that thought, came the fear that she meant nothing to him as a person. He'd have reacted the way he did to anyone who showed him kindness and compassion. She'd thought she was special to him. Well, she was. Truthfulness made her admit that. But she was special because she was the only one who fulfilled his human need for touch, not because of any inherently special characteristic of herself.

She'd always heard it was a bad idea to jump into bed with someone as soon as you met them. Now she knew why.

But Reynart had said he wouldn't expect her to want to have sex with him for at least two days. She'd use those two days to show him who she really was, so the next time they had sex, he'd be making love to *her*.

Something of her distress must have tensed the muscles in her hand, because he lifted his head and gazed down at her in concern. "Anjeli? Is something wrong?"

She couldn't possibly explain. And it wasn't like he'd lied to her or done anything wrong. He'd done everything right. Just for the wrong reason.

She sighed. She'd deal with that later. "Why'd you say you were going to disappoint me?"

"I must leave you. I will be expected to break my fast with the rest of the royal family and must not arrive after the King."

Her eyes widened, her gaze leaping to the scars on his chest as she wondered what the punishment was for keeping the King waiting. Putting both hands on his chest, she shoved Reynart away from her. "What are you waiting for, then? Go! I don't want you to get in trouble."

He nodded, refusing to meet her gaze, then tossed back the comforter and hopped out of bed. She shivered at the sudden chill and he quickly pulled the covers over her again, tucking her in. The thick layer of down was no substitute for his warm body beside her.

"Ah, Anjeli. Don't look at me that way. I must go."

"I said you should, didn't I?" She turned on her side facing away from him. And was glad she had, when she heard the unmistakable sounds of a chamber pot in use. She buried her flaming cheeks in the pillow.

She listened to him splashing water in a basin, then opening and closing the armoire. He grunted as he shoved his feet into a pair of boots, each heel striking the floor forcefully as he pulled the boots into place.

He walked back to the bed and she opened her eyes, thinking he intended to kiss her good-bye. Instead, he reached beneath his pillow and pulled out one of his black leather vambraces. Complete with two small, deadly looking knives.

Her eyes widened. "You slept with that? Under the pillow?"

Tightening the laces around his forearm, he nodded. He tied it, then tested the placement by flexing his arm, shooting first one, then the other knife into his cupped palm. "Of course."

"Do you always sleep with knives under the pillow?"

"No."

She sighed with relief.

Then he spoiled it by adding, "Usually I wear the vambraces to bed. But I didn't want to risk injuring you."

She blinked, remembering the ease with which those daggers had leapt to his hand in the stairwell and for what little cause. What if she'd been a restless sleeper and thrashed around in the night? A careless fling of her arm could have resulted in a knife in her back.

She'd never been so glad to be a quiet sleeper.

He brushed the back of his fingers along her jaw in a tender caress. "You need have no fear. I will keep you safe."

"Thank you." She forced a smile, although she suspected it was pale and sickly. Right now, she cared more about who would keep her safe from him.

He turned away, adjusting the loose cuffs of his tunic over his vambraces. "I brought you some meat from last night's dinner. I doubt I will be able to take more than a piece of fruit from the morning meal and, if anyone is watching me, I shall have to bring it to my horse. But luncheon is normally an individual meal, so I will be able to eat it here and share it with you."

"I can hold out until lunchtime." Her stomach gave the lie to her words, rumbling loudly. This talk of food was making her hungry. But first, she really needed to use that chamber pot and she wasn't about to do so with him still in the room.

* * * * *

Reynart entered the morning room to find Alaric gazing out the window toward the rose court. The servants had already laid out the trays of breakfast foods on one of the two narrow tables in the room; four varieties of meat, coddled eggs and a selection of fresh fruit, as well as a loaf of fresh bread and a second loaf sliced into cheese toast. Pots of tea steamed gently under their covers, the rich red preferred by most of the royal family as well as the dainty green tea the Queen affected as a sign of her culture and sophistication. The serving boy who would wait upon them this morning stood stiffly next to the table, at the moment a purely decorative accessory.

"You're late this morning." Alaric turned from the view, his eyes narrowing. "I thought you might have been ill."

"Concerned that the scratch you gave me yesterday might have festered?"

Alaric's gaze flicked to Reynart's upper arm. "Did it?"

"No. I powdered it on the practice field, as we were taught. We were also taught to always clean our weapons," Reynart reminded his brother, glad their swordmaster had been nowhere near the practice field, or the lesson would have been reinforced much more painfully.

Alaric flushed. "I cleaned my blade. After I left."

"Yes, you did leave in something of a hurry."

The flush turned an unhealthy purplish-red, but he didn't raise his voice. The serving boy would still have to strain to hear their soft conversation. "I didn't run away."

"I didn't say you did."

"You meant it, though. You thought I was so craven, I couldn't stand the sight of blood and had to flee."

"Regardless of what the Queen, your mother, insists on telling you, I have never thought you were a coward, Alaric. If you must know, I was looking for you after the match but you'd already gone to help Gervaise track down his missing experiment. Did he ever find it? Or is your pet mage careless with his own pets?"

Alaric's eyes widened briefly before narrowing, while the flush faded from his skin leaving him looking even paler than normal. "What do you know of Gervaise's experiment?" he demanded.

A direct blow. His brother needed to learn to mask his emotions better.

Reynart wondered what Alaric feared he knew. Certainly his brother couldn't know he had found the woman Gervaise was pursuing, and had hidden her in his own chambers.

Raising one brow in a convincing imitation of amused interest, Reynart answered, "The guard I spoke to said he had…misplaced a woman he was treating for a curse. Strange that I heard no rumor of any cursed noblewoman prior to this. Where was she from that her malady was not fodder for court gossip?"

"She wasn't a noblewoman."

"Indeed? I should think curing a commoner would be beneath the royal mage."

Alaric was saved from having to respond by the arrival of the King and Queen. The King took his usual seat at the head of the table, where he could watch the door. Reynart and Alaric sat on the sides, and the Queen sat at the foot, her back exposed to the door. Reynart occasionally wondered if at least part of her bitterness stemmed from the knowledge that her husband considered her the most expendable member of the family. Although admittedly, no one except Reynart had a reason to want her dead. Aside from her obsession with seeing her son named heir, she was a good Queen, probably a better Queen than his father was King. Not that Reynart would ever voice that sentiment.

The serving boy filled a plate for the King and presented it. The King nodded, silently pointing to various items for the boy to eat before he was satisfied the food was not poisoned. He waved the boy away.

The Queen was served next, although she only had the boy sample a token piece of bacon before dismissing him. Finally, the boy carried the remaining two plates to the table and presented them to the King. He chose the leftmost plate for Reynart and the rightmost plate for Alaric. The boy placed the chosen plates in front of the brothers, then carried over the teapots and tea glasses.

Again, the King silently selected which glass would be served to which person. Then the boy filled them. He sipped from the King's steaming glass, the King watching to ensure he actually swallowed some of the liquid.

The food's safety confirmed, the King began to eat. "Leave us now."

A cold chill ghosted over Reynart's flesh and he hesitated in the act of reaching for his tea. In his experience, the King's desire for privacy was never a good thing. Had he discovered his sons had been dueling yesterday?

"Reynart," the King said, stuffing a chunk of sausage into his mouth.

Reynart folded his hands in his lap. To eat while speaking to the King was an unforgivable sign of disrespect. "Yes, Your Majesty?"

"What qualities are needed for a good ruler?"

"A good ruler must be ruthless in exploiting advantages, determined and willing to try new things when the old no longer produce the required results."

"Like a marriage alliance for the barony of Sudern?"

"Yes, Your Majesty."

The King snorted in disgust and turned his attention to loading one of the coddled eggs onto a slice of cheese toast. Since he had not been formally excused, Reynart remained waiting, the enticing smell of hot meat and baked cheese making his mouth water. He'd expended a good deal of energy last night making love to Anjeli and he was very hungry.

"I don't like diplomacy," the King said at last, after he finished eating his egg. "Liars, the lot of them. No one lies to the point of a sword."

Reynart knew differently. One of the times he'd been on his knees before his father, looking up at the gleaming hand-and-a-half sword hovering before him with murderous intent, he'd started babbling, saying anything he could think of to keep that sword from falling. His father had wanted a confession from him, so he had invented a series of crimes on the spot. While serious, they were not the treasonous crime the King had originally believed him guilty of, so he merely whipped his son instead of killing him. He couldn't remember what the King thought he'd done or what he'd confessed to doing to appease him, but he remembered the lesson he'd learned. A clever lie hurt less than the truth. It was many years later before he learned that silence hurt even less and a clever silence hurt least of all.

He decided upon silence being the best course in this instance and waited for the King to continue. Eventually, he did.

"Still, it's possible the strategy might work. We lose nothing by trying it. I will also ready my forces for war. You have one week. Then tell me how the rebels will arrange their attacks." He glanced at his other son. "You have the same time to prepare a response for the barony's defenses."

Alaric bowed his head. "Yes, Your Majesty."

But Reynart did not immediately agree. Instead, he asked, "Your Majesty, may I inquire as to the purpose of this assignment?"

A hint of a flush tinted the King's cheeks and his hand gripped more tightly around his fork. "You will do as I tell you to do."

"Yes, Your Majesty. I just wondered if you were trying to determine how well we understand military strategy or if our suggestions might be used in the field."

The King lay down his fork, focusing his full attention on Reynart for the first time. "What difference would it make?"

"If the purpose of your assignment is to range my knowledge against Alaric's, I know his weaknesses and will adjust my strategy to capitalize upon them. I would use a different strategy against an unknown opponent."

The King laughed. "Ruthlessly exploit your advantages. Very good."

He stabbed his fork toward Alaric. "That's what you need to learn. Ruling a kingdom is about more than having the power to tell people what to do. It's knowing how to accomplish things so that you don't waste your power."

The Queen shifted restlessly, on the verge of protesting on her son's behalf, before subsiding into silence. No doubt she realized a protest now would only aggravate matters.

Alaric bowed his head again, this time to hide his flaming cheeks. "Yes, Your Majesty. I will remember that."

Reynart was filled with relief. The King had chosen the most generous interpretation of his question, praising him for his skill. He might as easily have decided Reynart was lazy, challenging his authority or simply stupid, all sins that would have earned stiff penalties. And the Queen had not found a way to twist the King's praise into condemnation.

The King returned to his breakfast, his gaze occasionally flicking up to Reynart. "I'm exploiting my advantage, too. You've got a slippery way of thinking, and so do those rebels. I want to see how you think they'll arrange their troops."

"I understand, Your Majesty."

"Good. Get started today."

Reynart smiled and bowed his head. "Yes, Your Majesty."

The King's challenge would be an enjoyable puzzle. But more than that, he now had a perfect excuse for spending the next few days in his rooms, reading up on Sudern and working out a troop strategy. If he could keep his mind and hands off of Anjeli long enough to do so.

Chapter Five

Angie's first surprise of the day was a pleasant one. The hammered brass chamber pot was somehow enchanted, so that it emptied whenever you closed the lid. She hoped she guessed correctly about the function of the absorbent squares of some felt-like substance stacked neatly on a shelf below the water basin, and that she hadn't just used something incredibly rare and expensive as toilet tissue.

Her second surprise was much less pleasing. Looking at the back of the dress she'd worn yesterday, she saw that the lacing started at the waist and threaded through every other hole to the top. When Reynart had undone the laces for her, he'd unlaced the return crossings, then loosened the rest. But the length of cord hanging out of the upper holes was not long enough to thread all the way back down to the waist of the dress. It would have to be tightened while she was wearing it. Maybe if the laces were in front she could have managed, but there was no way she could reach behind herself to do it, especially without a mirror. She couldn't possibly wear the dress.

Putting the dress back on the shelf where she'd stored it last night, she considered wearing just the chemise that she'd put on when she got out of bed. But it was too thin to provide any protection from the chill in the room. And she wasn't about to spend the whole day curled up underneath the comforter!

Instead, she searched through Reynart's armoire, figuring his closet was like anyone else's she'd ever known. The things he wore most frequently would be in the front and on the easy-to-reach shelves, while things that no longer fit or that were in need of repair would be tucked in back corners or fallen on the floor. Her search soon rewarded her with a dark green tunic he'd obviously outgrown. The sleeves fit her well if she turned back the cuffs and the bottom hem came to just above her knee.

One of the hooks in the tall half of the armoire contained a half-dozen different belts. Using the same strategy as before, she chose the one furthest to the back, which was a thin strip of chestnut brown leather with a single brass loop on one end. She looped the belt around her waist, converting Reynart's old shirt into a passable dress. After tugging the chemise up so that its extra fabric gathered above the belt, she knotted the belt in place. It would do.

After finding both of her slippers and putting them back on, she felt she was as dressed as she was going to be, so she went into the other room to find breakfast. She hadn't had any dinner the night before and she was starving.

She immediately spotted the lumpy, folded cloth sitting on the round table and unfolded it. It contained a thick slice of crusty bread that was covered with layered slices of meat. The meat looked like roast beef to her but she supposed it might be ox, or lamb, or any other animal that one roasted. That was topped with thick slices of a soft, pale yellow cheese.

Picking the sandwich apart, she tasted a bit of each element individually. The cheese was strong but not unpleasant. The roast meat was a little tougher than she was used to, and far too heavily spiced with pepper, but it was edible. She tried them together and discovered the cheese blunted the pepper taste, so she ate the rest of her meal as an open-faced sandwich.

After breakfast, she sat down with a comb and tried to work the snarls out of her hair to rebraid it. Grabbing the end of one undone braid in her fist, she was so busy attacking the hair with the comb that she didn't at first realize what was wrong. After all, it felt like her hair—thick, wavy and with an infuriating ability to snarl instantly. It was the right color. But there was too much of it.

She'd been trying to grow her hair back after having it in a trendy super-short cut. It was only down to her shoulder blades. This hair easily extended halfway down her back, once it was untwined from the complex braids that had bound it.

Having her hair transformed by whatever magical spell brought her here was more disturbing than simply being dressed in different clothing. She'd been wearing the standard outfit for a teenager—jeans, T-shirt and sneakers—and arrived wearing the standard outfit for a teenager in this place, according to Reynart's comments when they first met. That change made some kind of bizarre sense.

But her hair was part of herself. It was part of her identity. It might change over time but it would be a slow, gradual change, reflecting the underlying changes of her beliefs about what was fashionable, and whether or not the effort that went into keeping her hair stylish could be better spent on other things that mattered more.

Her musings were interrupted by the rattle of the doorknob. Instantly, she jumped to her feet and ran back into the bedroom. She could hide in the armoire.

"Anjeli?" Reynart called softly, followed by a loud thud.

She stopped trying to cram herself into the upright portion of the armoire and hurried back out to the sitting room. A stack of heavy books were piled on top of the table.

Reynart had turned to face her when she entered the room and now stood there, staring at her with wide eyes, his mouth half-open as whatever he'd been about to say died unspoken. Finally, he swallowed and managed to ask huskily, "What are you wearing?"

"One of your old shirts. You don't mind, do you? I couldn't figure out how to do up the laces on the dress by myself."

"Not at all." He shook his head, both emphasizing his words and seeming to break himself out of the stupor that had claimed him since he saw her. Pointing to the books, he added, "I need to research one of our more troublesome provinces. I thought you might be interested."

She took one eager step toward the pile of books before she remembered her discovery of the day before. "I am. But I can't read your books."

"It's all right. We can—"

"No. I mean, I *can't* read your books. The words just look like funny squiggles to me."

His expression took on the peculiar shuttered look she was coming to recognize meant he'd been surprised. "You said yesterday you could read."

"I can. In English. I just can't read whatever language these—" She flung out one hand in a sweeping gesture that included the books on the table as well as the ones on his desk. "—are written in."

"It's a mix of Tsieche and Illornian." Frowning, he dug through the books, selecting two and laying them on the table before her. "Which looks more like your Ingless?"

She flipped open both books. One was written in the same flowing script she'd been unable to decipher yesterday. The other had a recognizable alphabet, although the letters were not quite the ones she was used to, as if Greek or Norse letters had been included instead of the standard Roman set. She pointed.

"That one."

"Illornian." His frown deepened. "But we are speaking a Tsieche dialect."

Very carefully, with precise pronunciation that made him sound almost British, he asked, "Can you understand me?"

She nodded. "Yes. But you have an accent you don't normally have."

Once again, he asked her a carefully phrased question. But this time, he was clearly speaking another language.

"I'm sorry. I have no idea what you just said."

Reynart pulled out one of the chairs and sat down at the table. When she reached for the other chair, he caught her hand and pulled her toward him instead. "Sit on my lap. I'm going to teach you to read."

Smiling, she sat sideways across his legs, one arm loosely wrapped around his shoulders. Her makeshift dress slid up, leaving the backs of her thighs naked against the rough weave of his hose. She felt his powerful leg muscles shifting as he adjusted his position slightly, nudging her to a more comfortable spot pressed against his body. The warm ridge of his cock stirred to life beside her thigh but he seemed determined to ignore his body's response, reaching past Angie to pull the book closer to where they could both see it.

Then he began to read.

The story was intriguing, being a legend of the Amin-Te, which Angie roughly translated as the washerwomen of death. These women would appear to heroes going out into battle as the men passed over rivers, silently washing their bloody clothes in the flowing water. From this, the heroes would know they were going to die in the upcoming battle. They could take any steps necessary to ensure a smooth inheritance of their lands and property, and commit their wishes and feelings to paper for their loved ones to read after their death. This particular legend described one Severne, a hero of great renown, who, upon passing one of these washerwomen, leapt off of his horse and jumped into the river to confront her. She was so impressed by his daring that she held out the tunic she was washing, allowing him to see the spear hole in the side. During the battle that followed, one of the enemies did indeed hurl a spear at Severne but the hero turned away at the last instant, changing the mortal wound into a merely grievous wound.

"Did he live?" Angie asked in a hushed whisper.

"What Severne did not know," Reynart continued reading, "was that his enemy had tipped his spear with poison. Had the blow been allowed to fall as originally intended he would have died instantly. Instead, he suffered for three agonizing days. But while he was dying, he continued to lead his army and defeated the barbarian invaders mere hours before finally succumbing to the poison."

"That's horrible!"

Reynart tilted his head to look at her, one eyebrow raised questioningly. "Why?"

"The Amin-Te warned him about the spear but didn't warn him about the poison. He suffered three days of agony and still died."

"Of course he died. She couldn't show him anything that would stop his death, because then there would be no reason for her to appear."

"Well then, what was the point? Are the Amin-Te some kind of evil spirits?"

"No, they're not evil. They're the handmaidens of Lady Death, just as the Amin-Re are the warriors of Lord Death. She offers merciful death, while he offers untimely death. To die quickly in battle is both."

Angie shivered and cuddled closer to Reynart, nestling her head in the hollow of his shoulder. Softly, she pressed a kiss against his throat. When he didn't protest, she kissed him again.

The arm that had been loosely encircling her, pressing lightly against her back while he turned the pages of the book, tightened and he moved his hand from the tabletop to her hip. He nudged aside the scrap of shirttail still covering her legs and slipped his hand along her bare thigh.

She sighed deeply, hoping he'd slide his hand between her thighs and touch her as he had last night. Or turn her so that she was straddling his waist and let his eager cock move inside her again. She'd had every intention of making him prove he recognized her individuality before making love again but, after listening to his sexy voice reading to her and feeling his hand stroking her skin, her body was humming with desire, tiny electric sparks tingling where he touched her and making her forget everything but the feelings he roused in her and the need to feel him again.

Reynart had more self-restraint.

He sighed deeply, his hand lightly squeezing her thigh. Then he reached for the book and pulled it closer.

Angie sighed, too, and abandoned kissing him. Instead, she leaned against his chest and listened to the steady beat of his heart.

"So what are you studying this for, anyway? You seemed to know all about the Amin-Te already."

"This was a legend about Severne, a folk hero of the province my father is having trouble with. He wants me to predict how the rebels will attack in the spring."

She twisted to look up into his face. "How will reading an old legend help?"

He grinned, the light in his eyes dazzling her. "It's not just an old legend. It's part of the people's culture. A culture that believes that a hero should be willing to suffer three days of excruciating agony in order to lead his side to victory. That's quite different from a culture whose hero would have found a way to cheat death entirely or one where the warrior would have been struck down instantly for daring to confront the Amin-Te and challenge fate. They will all plan their battles differently, having vastly different definitions of heroism."

Angie considered this, running her fingertips back and forth across Reynart's shoulder as she thought.

Eventually, he reached up and clasped her hand, stopping her absentminded caresses.

"What?" she asked.

"You are far too potent a distraction, milady," he whispered.

He lifted her hand away from his shoulder, then selected another book from the table, giving it to her to hold.

She opened it and found it contained a series of detailed hand-inked drawings, describing the towns and castles of the province. There was also a map, showing the castles at the centers of overlapping concentric rings.

"What's this?"

"Each of the castles has varying areas it can defend. The smallest circle indicates the area that can be protected by archers from within the castle walls. The medium circle represents the area that can be protected by soldiers who will come out of the castle to fight. And the largest circle indicates how far the castle's mounted soldiers can travel to protect it. My brother is planning the defense of the castles. My task is to determine how the rebels will try to take them."

She leaned forward to study the map. "Why take them at all? Why not just attack the soldiers when they come out?"

"The rebels do not have enough men to stage a siege." Reynart was no longer looking at the map, his gaze captured by the view of her cleavage exposed when she bent forward. Hesitantly, he reached up and cupped one of her breasts.

Angie closed her eyes and arched into his palm.

His thumb flicked lightly back and forth, teasing her nipple to tingling awareness. Groaning softly, he bent his head and kissed her throat, the curve of her shoulder and the exposed vee of her chest.

"You must rest today," he whispered, sounding as if he was trying to convince himself as well as reminding her. "And I must study all of these books, to prepare an acceptable proposal for the King."

She eyed the less-than-tidy pile of books through half-open eyes. "How long do you have?"

"Until the end of the week."

"You can't possibly read this many books by then!"

Reynart stopped kissing her. A faint shiver passed through him and he reached for the book of legends again. "I must."

"Read the next legend out loud and I'll try to pay more attention to the words this time. I think I'm starting to get the connection between the letters and the words. Once I understand it, I can help you read some of these books."

He nodded to the book she was holding. "There are other maps in there. Do you see anything that looks like where you are from?"

Chewing her lip in thought, Angie flipped through the pages, recognizing as the province of Sudern became part of the island labeled Suddalyk. That was part of a two-island chain labeled Nord D'Rae, which was to the west of a large land mass labeled Illornian Empire. If she squinted and held her head at an angle, it sort of almost looked like Italy. Or what she imagined Italy looked like. Her grasp of geography had never been particularly strong.

The larger landmass that contained the Illornian Empire, however, looked only vaguely like Europe, being more broad than it was tall. And there was nothing that looked anything like North America.

Her faint hope that she was just in a strangely altered corner of the familiar world, or perhaps in the distant past, vaporized.

"No. None of this looks familiar."

"Can you draw your land?"

She thought for a moment, then nodded. Reynart reluctantly lifted her off of his lap and went to get something to write with from his desk. He returned with a thin piece of hard gray chalk and a slate. One of those absorbent felt squares had been bunched up and tied into a puff and the thread had been attached to the wooden frame of the slate.

He handed her the slate and chalk, then stood beside her, watching, as she carefully drew something vaguely resembling the United States. She didn't think Florida stuck out quite so much like a thumb and she was pretty sure Washington and Maine were not supposed to look like mirror images of each other. But it was recognizably the United States.

Reynart frowned at it. "It looks like a cooking pot with a broken leg."

He pointed to California and the obvious lack of a proper leg to offset Texas and Florida.

"There's something else there." She quickly sketched in Mexico, hinting at the curving lines of Central America. "But that's another country, so I didn't draw it."

Reynart shook his head. "I do not recognize it. How many cities are in your country?"

"Good grief, how should I know? Thousands, I guess."

His eyes widened. "Thousands of cities? That would be hundreds of thousands of people."

"Millions actually."

"*Millions* of people? How large is this land?"

"Ummm…it's pretty big. Two or three thousand miles across, I think." At his blank look, she tried another frame of reference. "There was a fellow who walked from coast to coast a while back. It took him a little over six months."

"Six months. To walk across it." He blinked, obviously struggling to come to terms with a single country of such great size. "And one king rules the entire country?"

"Yes." She took pity on him and didn't try to explain the concept of a democracy to his already overburdened brain.

Slowly, he sat down, his eyes fixed on the slate. Almost without conscious thought, he gathered her into his arms and pulled her onto his lap again.

"You understand spoken words, but not written ones, yet you handle a slate pencil with the familiarity of someone who learned to write years ago. You are clearly intelligent, yet you lack even the most basic knowledge of our customs and beliefs. I know every country in the world and the land you describe does not match any of them. Yesterday, I might have thought you were lying but I believe I know you well enough now to know you are telling me the truth about this land of yours." He let out his breath in a sigh and absent-mindedly began stroking her thigh again. "Although I do not understand how it is possible, the mage Gervaise must have brought you to us from another world."

* * * * *

They continued reading, with Anjeli's warm body cuddled against his to provide a tempting distraction. He couldn't keep his hands off of her. Even when he was wholly engrossed in a particular legend, recounting of a battle or description of a location that he was reading about, he held her close, his hand straying from the pages of the book to caress her thigh. Sometimes he would duck his chin, just to feel the brush of her hair against his skin.

She'd given up trying to follow the words in the books as he read, claiming it was giving her a headache, and instead sat curled against him, her soft breath caressing his neck and occasionally stealing down the open front of his tunic to tease his chest. She listened to him read or, when he fell silent to rest his voice or make notes on his slate, she watched him.

Their awareness of each other hummed between them, unspoken and unacknowledged, yet ever present. He knew her as completely as a man could know a woman, and yet, he knew her not at all. Normally, the mystery that surrounded her would make him tense and suspicious, alert for possible danger and anticipating an attack. Yet with Anjeli, he didn't care. He was as completely happy as he could ever remember being. If it took him a lifetime to learn her secrets, he would be content.

He could not hide her in his rooms indefinitely. In an atmosphere where secrets carried the highest currency, sooner or later someone would guess that he had a lover sharing his suite. The news would travel to the King and Queen and Reynart would be forced to confess. He didn't want to think about Anjeli's fate if that should happen.

But he didn't need to hide her indefinitely. Ladria would be returning any day now and he felt certain his sister would help him to find a solution. Perhaps she could appoint Anjeli as her maid. The two women would get along very well together. If Gervaise was still looking for her, Ladria could use her magic to conceal Anjeli while they smuggled her out of the castle, to a home in the city. Reynart would no longer be able to see her every day but he could still see her frequently.

His arms tightened around her.

The knock at his door startled them both. Silently, he lifted her to her feet and nodded at the bedroom. She scampered out of the room, leaving him to loudly drag his chair from the table and walk to his door. Dagger at the ready, he opened the door from the side.

A serving girl stood in the hall, holding a cloth-covered tray by its handles and taking some of its weight onto her out-flung hip. She straightened immediately when the door edged open, dropping into an awkward curtsey to present the tray.

"My lord Prince, I have brought your lunch."

He glanced up and down the empty hall, then opened the door for her. "Place it on the table."

She rose to her feet, the perfectly level tray never wavering, and entered the room, her eyes downcast and head bent. He closed and bolted the door behind her, out of habit.

"Have I your permission to move your books to make a place for the tray, my lord Prince?"

He'd thought it could be squeezed into the empty area of the table, but one of the piles of books looked perilously close to tipping and, no doubt, she feared upsetting it. He grabbed the offending pile and transferred it to the chair.

"There's room now."

"Yes, my lord Prince." She arranged the tray, pulling off the cloth to reveal a plate of cold meat and cheese, a bowl containing two marbled plums and a dusty pink apple and half a loaf of bread. A pot of red tea steamed beside a flagon of afternoon ale, flanked by an empty tea glass and goblet.

The servant folded her hands before her, bowing her head, and waited for additional orders. Unlike the rest of his family, Reynart saw no reason to make the servants taste food for poison. He could recognize the symptoms of all the known poisons and choose the correct antidote to any contaminant in his food with plenty of time to spare before he fell prey to it. There were practical as well as tactical advantages to having been trained by an assassin.

"That will be all. I'll leave the tray outside when I'm done, along with the ewer of water. It needs refilling."

She bobbed a curtsey. "Yes, my lord Prince."

As she moved toward the door, he took one of the plums and bit into it. The flesh was firm yet not hard, a layer of sweetness with a sharp, tangy center.

"The plums are excellent. Bring a bowl of them when you refill the ewer."

"Yes, my lord Prince. Shall I knock?"

"No. Just leave them." He would probably be at sword practice when she arrived with the fruit. The hall guard would ensure that no one tampered with the fruit in his absence, except perhaps Alaric, who might steal a few plums.

The serving girl hesitated by the door and Reynart set down the half-eaten plum to unbolt the door and show her out. All the servants knew better than to touch his door without his permission, after the traps had burned two of them. He frowned, bolting the door again after the girl left. He would have to impress upon Anjeli the importance of remaining within his suite.

He turned to find Anjeli already at the table, eyeing the food hungrily. "Come on. I'm starved!"

Laughing, he resumed his seat, pleased when she climbed into his lap again rather than using the other chair. "Shall I feed you, milady, and satisfy your hunger?"

She closed her eyes and sighed, her breath softly caressing the underside of his jaw. "One of my hungers, anyway."

Tipping her head up with one finger, he bent his own head and captured her lips, nibbling them as delicately as if she was a sweet, juicy plum whose skin he did not wish to break. Her breath hitched, then she moaned into his mouth, her tongue darting out to taste the sweetness of the plum juice on his lips.

Their tongues tangled, tasting and stroking, as their mouths met and moved apart in a gentle dance. With one hand, Reynart caressed her smooth thigh, his spear rising to press against her other leg. He trailed his other fingers along her brow and down her jawline, then pulled aside the loose neck of his old tunic to expose her breast to his questing hand.

Anjeli arched into his palm, twining the fingers of her hand with his at her hip and crushing his palm against her. Her remaining hand burrowed into his hair, molding her palm to the shape of his skull and holding his lips pressed tight to hers.

Then her stomach rumbled. They broke apart, laughing.

"It seems, milady, I must feed you quickly or risk the direst of consequences."

She grinned and nipped playfully at his ear. "Or you just don't know what I might eat."

His spear rose to full battle readiness at her teasing words but he did not dare allow himself to indulge in any of her charms. Or he knew he'd be carrying her into his bedroom to storm her keep again, and he had sworn to give her the two days he'd been assured a virgin would need. She would forgive him for hurting her in their mutual passion-blindness. But he would never forgive himself.

Instead, he held her and fed her selected nibbles from the tray of food before them. Cutting up the apple, he layered the honey-flavored wedges with mellow, smoky cheese, tasting the first himself and then placing them one after another between her lips. He piled thick slabs of last night's roast on crusty slices of bread and they tore into them, showering each other with sprays of crumbs.

Anjeli poured herself a glass of tea but he caught her hand before she could lift the tea to her lips.

"Wait."

He slipped out from under her and retrieved the golden goblet Ladria had given him from its place on the shelf. While he might know all the symptoms and counteragents for poisons, she did not. After pouring the tea into the goblet and letting it sit the required thirty heartbeats, he decanted it into the tea glass and handed it to her.

"It's safe to drink now."

She eyed the tea suspiciously. "And it wasn't before?"

"One never knows." He shrugged. "Caution takes little extra time and it is time well spent should you ever have need of it."

"So how did pouring the tea into that cup first help?"

"My sister enchanted it, to neutralize poisons." He filled the goblet with ale from the flagon and took a deep swallow. "She may not be a particularly powerful mage but she is truly gifted at binding spells to objects."

Anjeli's eyes widened. "The chamber pot was another one of her gifts?"

"Yes." He grinned. "I am the only member of the royal family so honored. The King distrusts magic and would not allow an enchanted item so close to his private parts. And Ladria would never give anything to the Queen or Alaric."

"She doesn't like them?"

Reynart hesitated, a lifetime of caution preventing him from speaking the simple truth, that his sister hated the Queen and resented her son. "She feels it would be disloyal to the memory of her mother, the first Queen, to accept the second Queen and her son."

Anjeli frowned. "When did her mother die?"

"About a week after she was born. Complications from the birth." It had long been rumored that the King had killed his first Queen when the infant Ladria's binding ceremony indicated the baby had magical aptitudes. The Nord D'Rae royal line did not breed mages. Knowing his father, Reynart had no trouble believing the King had flown into a murderous rage upon learning of his daughter's "defect."

"Then she never knew her mother. How would it be disloyal to her memory to care for her stepmother?"

Reynart stared at Anjeli, amazed that she could even ask the question. That alone showed what a strange place she must be from.

He handed her the marbled plum and shifted the topic of conversation. "I requested a bowl of these to be brought up. That will give you something to eat while I'm at dinner. The serving girl will most likely bring them up while I'm at sword practice and leave them outside."

Anjeli bit into the plum, juice trickling down her chin. He longed to lick it away and thought happily of all the wonderful things that could be done with an entire bowl of plums. Instead, she wiped away the juice with the back of her hand.

"What do you mean, sword practice? I thought you had to read all these books."

"Yes, I do. But not at the cost of my military skills. Alaric and I will both have our usual two hours with the swordmaster."

"Two hours? But what am I supposed to do while you're gone?"

He considered. Obviously, she could not read. "Can you sew?"

"What, you mean like embroidery?"

"Ladria spends as many hours sewing and practicing with needle and thread as I do working with sword, shield and knife. Embroidering tapestries and decorating clothing, yes, but also repairing tears and holes."

Anjeli smiled, the expression brightening her entire face. "I can't do anything fancy. But I can mend a seam and fix a tear. Do you have a lot that needs mending?"

"More than enough to keep you busy." He gestured toward the overflowing basket, chuckling as her eyes widened and her mouth gaped. "My sister has been gone for many weeks."

"Don't your servants do that? I always sort of thought maids did the mending and princesses would just sew pretty, decorative tapestries."

"The servants would sew my clothing, if I trusted them enough to allow them to do so. But since I don't and Ladria likes a wide variety of needlework on which to practice, she does it for me."

Anjeli shook her head. "I'm not even going to ask what you think they could do to your clothes that you refuse to trust them. I'm just glad your paranoia will give me something to keep myself busy with."

"I'll get a needle and thread for you from Ladria's room." He smiled, recalling what else he could find in Ladria's room. She kept a jar of powder that would prevent pregnancies, so that she suffered no unwanted complications from her discreet and quickly ended affairs. That would be highly useful tomorrow night, when it was once again safe for him to bed Anjeli.

Chapter Six

Angie spent the afternoon sewing by the light of the open window, carefully mending the rents and tears in Reynart's clothing so that they could not be seen. She was alarmed at how many of them were accompanied by what appeared to be bloodstains.

She reached for the next tunic and gasped in dismay as she shook it out. A reddish brown cloud of dried blood flaked away from the material. Turning it over, she saw that the back was covered with blood. Not in a solid pattern, but in black stripes where the blood had completely soaked through the fabric, fading to rusty patches between them.

She smoothed her hand across the stiff tunic, tears springing to her eyes. Unbidden, she saw again the smooth white scars that marred Reynart's chest. How many marred his back? They could not be discerned by touch and, when she'd seen his naked back, it had been too dark to make out any details. But for this shirt to be in his mending pile, he had to have covered his raw wounds with it within the past few weeks. Surely such a recent injury must still pain him but he'd shown no sign of it.

Eventually she found the reason the tunic had been added to the mending. One cuff had been torn half-off. She wondered how. Had he been trying to get away from something or someone?

She heard the door open and close softly, then Reynart was on his knees beside her, lifting her tearstained face so he could see her. Even with his black hair spiky with sweat and a fine layer of dust covering him, he was the most beautiful man she'd ever seen. That someone would hurt him on purpose... She choked back another sob.

"Anjeli? What is wrong?"

Mutely, she held up the tunic. His forehead creased and, hesitantly, he ventured, "The tunic cannot be repaired?"

The tears flowed faster, obscuring her vision. Was he so frequently a bloody mess that he no longer found it worth commenting upon?

She took a deep, steadying breath. "Of course the tunic can be repaired. It's only a torn cuff. What about you? Isn't this your blood soaked through it?"

"Oh. The King summoned Gervaise to repair the damage to me." He took the tunic from her shaking hands and tossed it away, as if removing it from her sight could make her forget what she had seen. But those were not battle wounds or other accidental injuries. They were the evenly spaced marks of deliberate violence, of cold-hearted torture and abuse.

"Why?" she choked out.

It was the wrong question. Reynart's face immediately assumed the closed expression she knew so well. He stood, then pulled her to her feet.

"I must wash and change for dinner. If you get hungry before I return, the servants have brought a bowl of plums." He reached into the center of the bowl and removed a marbled plum.

It burst as he bit into it, smearing his dusty face with juice. He held out the half-eaten plum to her, his tongue darting out to sweep the sweet juice from his lips.

"They are delicious."

She accepted the sticky plum, nibbling carefully around the pit. It was delicious. And he was changing the subject.

She followed him into his bedroom and watched as he stripped off the dusty practice clothing. Unselfconsciously naked, except for the leather vambraces laced around his forearms, his body was a finely muscled sculpture. She felt herself growing weak with desire, her bones dissolving and mist invading her brain. She needed to press herself tightly against him, seeking his strength, because she no longer had any.

When he turned to pour water into the basin beside his bed, she gasped. Not because of the dozen thin white scars that decorated his back, but because his scars were a mixture of angles and lengths. He bore no evenly spaced lines that would have matched the wounds beneath his bloodstained tunic.

He glanced over his shoulder, frowned, then turned back to the more important task of washing away the dust and sweat. "If you want to make yourself useful," he said, between splashes of water, "knock the dust off the practice clothes so that I can hang them up."

Dutifully, Angie pounded the practice clothing, hitting the defenseless garments with all of her built-up frustration, choking as the cloud of dust rose up to engulf her. Wet arms enfolded her, pulling her back against his sleek body.

"Not so hard," he murmured into her ear, then kissed her neck. His cock was soon extremely hard.

He pushed the hem of her tunic out of the way, sliding his heavy warmth up behind her, until the thick ridge of his erection nestled in the valley between her ass cheeks. He ground against her and she whimpered softly, loving the feel of him pressing against her but aching for his cock to be pressing inside her. Liquid heat pulsed deep within her, ready to ease his way along her passage.

"Storm my castle," she whispered. "The portcullis is already raised and the moat is flooding."

He groaned, tightening his arms around her. "No. You must rest today and tonight."

"Says who?" she demanded petulantly. She wanted him inside her. Now. And she knew that's where he wanted to be, too. It was a stupid rule to make them wait.

"I do." He guided her backward, then stepped away and pushed her down onto the bed. "Sit."

Not certain what he wanted, she sat where she'd landed on the soft feather comforter. Was he asking her to keep out of his way to allow him to finish dressing for dinner?

She watched in confusion as he bent and picked up his padded practice tunic, folded it over, then placed it on the floor beside the bed and knelt on it. He pulled her forward, until she sat on the very edge of the bed, her knees spread to either side of his shoulders. He lifted the hems of her tunic and chemise, tucking them up beneath her belt and exposing her to his view.

"You are beautiful," he whispered, his voice husky with desire.

Angie held her breath, hopeful yet fearful at the same time. Reynart's strong hands caressed her thighs, then slid up to cup her backside. Holding her in place, he bent his head and kissed the hot flesh between her legs.

She gasped, warm liquid welling forth, even as she instinctively tried to jerk away from the unexpected touch. But his hands caressed and soothed, holding her firmly so that she could not escape. And as soon as the initial surprise faded, she had no wish to be anywhere other than where she was.

Sensing her relaxation, Reynart began his slow assault on her keep. His tongue found the concealed resting place of her barbican, circling around it until the tower stood tall. Then he slipped his lips around it, suckling and kissing while his tongue teased its roof.

She moaned, clenching her fingers in the damp strands of his thick hair and tipping her hips to allow him even greater access to her secrets. His fingers kneaded the globes of her backside while he kissed and suckled, filling her with fire.

"More," she whispered.

Obedient to her command, he nipped lightly at her barbican, just a gentle squeezing of his teeth. But it ignited a firestorm within her, powerful lightning crackling from synapse to synapse until she shook and cried out.

She thought he'd be finished then, but he'd only started. He pressed his face deeper into the damp hair between her legs and found her wide-open portcullis with his mouth. His tongue swept out, lapping up the liquid that had already trickled forth.

They groaned in unison.

Then his tongue pressed inside. She winced as he touched the flesh still tender from last night's exertions and admitted sourly that he'd been right not to try thrusting his hard cock inside her. But that thought soon spiraled away in a haze of pleasant sensation as his tongue gently fondled her, teasing her to another gasping pinnacle of pleasure. He held her there, shaking and begging for release, until she thought she might go insane if he didn't finish with her. Then his mouth closed over her portcullis, sucking hard, as his tongue plunged deep, flicking in and out over and over again, ever faster, until she wrapped her legs around his shoulders and arched backward, thrusting her hips up and screaming his name as she flooded his mouth with her release.

When she returned to her senses, she found he'd shifted their positions slightly, so that she was lying across the comforter with her legs hanging over the side, and he was resting with his head in her lap, eyes closed and a faint smile on his lips.

She sat up slowly, careful not to disturb him. He made a soft sound of protest, his loose arm around her hips tightening. Long seconds of silence stretched into minutes as she watched his chest rise and fall with his even breathing, until the weight of her gaze caused him to stir.

He looked up at her through half-lidded eyes, a smug smile of male confidence on his lips. Angie giggled. He looked so pleased with himself, she couldn't help it.

Distant bells tolled and he reluctantly rose to his feet. "I must dress for dinner."

The bells had rung yesterday as they'd been sneaking in to his rooms, too, and he'd dressed in a hurry. But they'd been ringing on and off all day and she'd never heard them chime the hour. "Do you use the bells to tell time?"

He nodded as he pulled on charcoal colored hose. "Yes. The temples mark the hours, with services held every three. So that is when they ring the bells, inviting people to join them in celebrating the worship of the Heavenly Pair."

"But how do you know which bell is ringing? They all sound the same."

His voice muffled by the tunic and undertunic he was pulling over his head, Reynart answered, "Just look out the window. It is later than mid-afternoon and not yet night. So it must be the *Saezar* bell ringing."

The layers of dark gray and burgundy satin and velvet settled into place. Tonight, his tunic was accented with embroidered pieces of jet and he selected a matching pair of velvet shoes.

"It grows more confusing in bad weather," he admitted. "But I've always found my stomach to be remarkably accurate at tallying the passing candlemarks."

Angie laughed. "So that must be the dinner bell, because you're hungry."

He turned toward her with a frown. "Will you be hungry? The plums are not much."

"I had a big lunch." Indeed, he'd let her eat most of it. "Besides, it will be getting too dark to see, soon. I'll probably just go to bed early."

"There are candles on the desk, if you'd like to stay awake until I return."

"Okay."

They shared a brief, lingering kiss, then he hurried out of the room. She found the candles, neatly stacked in a drawer, and a mirror-backed candleholder that would increase and focus the light for reading. Except, of course, that she couldn't read any of his books. And she'd lost her heart for sewing.

She ate most of the plums, leaving a few for breakfast tomorrow. Then she combed out her hair again and rebraided it in two long plaits. After undressing and hanging her clothes in the armoire for tomorrow, she washed up and crawled into bed to wait for Reynart.

She didn't mean to fall asleep but she woke in darkness to find him sliding gingerly between the sheets. She started to roll over to face him but his arm tightened around her, pinning her in place.

"It's late," he muttered, his usually clear voice strangely thick. "Go back to sleep."

Wriggling backwards, she snuggled up against him. Something felt wrong, though, and, after a moment, she realized his normally eager cock was not showing the least sign of interest.

"Reynart?"

"Sleep, Anjeli."

She tried, although how he expected her to be able to fall asleep with his arm like a vice around her ribs, she had no idea. Behind her, his breathing deepened. He didn't quite snore but the warm puffs of air that gusted across her shoulder blades were annoyingly loud.

The last thing she remembered before finally drifting back to sleep was the sound of the midnight bells, incongruously jubilant in the velvety darkness. Six hours later, the dawn bells woke her from her restless sleep.

Reynart had drawn his legs up as he slept and, as she was in front of him, she'd been squashed into a sort of semi-fetal position during the night. Her legs were cramped and she still couldn't breathe.

She grabbed his arm with both hands, intending to lift it away. Instantly, the iron band tightened around her and he sat up, dragging her with him. A dagger flashed in his other hand as he tensed, alert for any threat.

Shoving at his arm, she struggled to push him away before she blacked out from lack of oxygen. He released her, the dagger disappearing back under the pillow where it came from, and she rounded on him in fury.

"What the hell—?" She stopped, staring in shock at his face. No wonder he'd had trouble speaking and breathing. A raised red welt scored from the middle of his cheek to the opposite jaw, slicing across his mouth. His upper lip had split and the regal planes of his face were distorted by swelling.

He turned his head away, unable to meet her gaze. "Forgive me, milady. I do not react well to waking suddenly."

"Do you have ice you can put on that? Or a steak?" No, steaks were for black eyes. Although, since she'd never understood why a slab of meat was supposed to be an effective cure, she had no idea whether or not it would work for a split lip.

Realizing she was close to babbling, Angie took a deep breath. She wouldn't ask him what had happened. If he wanted to tell her, she'd listen. But she wouldn't increase his suffering by prying. And in the meantime, she'd do whatever she could to alleviate his pain.

He nodded, carefully. "There's a salve. Blue and gold jar. Second shelf."

Pushing aside the fallen covers, Angie crawled out of bed. In the rosy glow of dawn creeping through the narrow window, she searched the ceramic jars on his shelves using only her eyes, her hands clasped tightly behind her back. He'd warned her before not to touch anything on the shelves, and while he wouldn't have told her to get the jar of salve if it wasn't safe to touch, the same could not be said for the jars around it. His stories of what had happened to the servants foolish enough to disobey his wishes and touch his things had impressed upon her the lesson that nothing in these rooms was safe unless he told her it was safe.

The blue and gold jar was a low, wide jar of deep cobalt, painted in gold with a stylized representation of some winged creature. She checked one more time to be sure that no other jar was also blue and gold, then grabbed it and hurried back into the bedroom.

While she'd been gone, Reynart had already gotten up and gotten dressed and was now sitting on the end of the bed, waiting for her. She frowned.

"Won't this be messy? It might stain."

"It will be fine."

He held out his hand for the salve and she noticed he only moved the lower part of his arm, keeping his shoulder absolutely still. She swallowed, her fingers clutching the jar.

"Your face isn't the only place you were hit, is it?"

"The salve, Anjeli."

"Is it?"

They glared at each other but his shadowed eyes lacked heat and his gaze quickly dropped before hers. He mumbled, "No."

She took a deep breath, willing herself to be strong and not react no matter what she might see.

"Take off your shirt."

"I only need the salve for my lip."

"Take off your shirt."

Again, Reynart dropped his gaze first. Slowly, as if hoping she might yet change her mind, he lifted the tunic to the middle of his ribs. He paused, breathing deeply, and she sensed he was steeling himself for the ordeal ahead. Then he pulled the tunic over his head, hissing as he raised his arms and pulled the skin across his shoulders.

Silently, he turned so that his back was facing her. She bit her lip. It wasn't as bad as it could have been. But it was bad enough.

Long red welts crisscrossed his back, six in each direction. The marks of violence stood out vividly against his pale skin. There wasn't any bleeding, or even bruising, but where the welts crossed, raised knots had formed.

"How do I apply the salve?"

"Rub it on. Gently. It takes down swelling."

She opened the jar, choking as the wave of mentholated fumes hit her nose. Whatever else was in the thick yellow salve, she knew one ingredient.

Dipping her fingers into the jar, she scooped up a glop of salve. Carefully, she pressed it to the very edge of the first welt, then smoothed the salve over his swollen skin. Reynart hissed, stiffening his back, but otherwise made no protest. When she started on the second welt, he silently clenched his fists in the comforter.

"How are you doing?" she asked, after she finished smearing the line of salve down his back.

"Talk to me. Tell me of your world."

So she told him about her home in Arizona, about her high school and about Christmas shopping at the mall. She had no idea how much of what she said he was following but her words gave him something to concentrate upon other than the pain and that was enough.

Finally, she was done. The salve seemed to be doing its job, since Reynart already held himself less stiffly.

Climbing up onto the bed, she knelt before him to apply the salve to his face. His gaze flicked briefly to hers before he looked down, studiously intent upon the rumpled comforter clutched in his hands.

His shame was harder to bear than the physical injuries. At least those would heal in time. Gently, she smoothed the salve onto his cheek.

"I don't know what happened last night and you don't have to tell me if you don't want to. I just want you to know, in case you've got some macho tough-guy thing going on, I don't think any less of you for it."

The look in his eyes could have melted the most frozen of hearts. All the hope he did not dare to voice burned in their emerald depths, although it was still overshadowed by fear.

"I spoke out of turn," Reynart whispered.

Angie stared at him in horrified disbelief. "Your father whaled on you like this for interrupting him?"

"Not for interrupting. Speaking out of turn." He paused, struggling to find a way to explain it to someone who had no knowledge of the convoluted political atmosphere in which he lived, then gave up and shook his head. "He called on me to remain silent and I did not."

His lips turned in a wry smile, quirking up on the undamaged side of his face. "That's why he made sure to hit me on the mouth. So I'd remember to keep it closed next time."

Angie snorted. "I hope he doesn't treat the rest of the country the way he treats his family, or—"

His hand shot out, grabbing her wrist in a painfully tight hold that shocked her into silence. "Milady, you promised. Speak no word against the King. You promised."

"But—"

"You promised."

She could no longer feel her fingers. "Okay. I promise."

He released her. Trying to shake some feeling back into her fingers, she muttered, "But I can think it."

"No, milady. Do not even think it." Reynart gestured at his swollen face. "This was a reminder, nothing more. I have seen him angry. You would not survive."

His gaze turned inward, taking on a haunted cast, and Angie knew he had not simply seen the King angry, he'd been the target of that anger. Probably more than once. He knew what it cost to survive.

Silently, she resolved that he would never have to endure that kind of pain again. Or at least, he would not have to endure it alone.

He rose slowly to his feet and crossed to his armoire. "There's no disguising the smell of the salve but if I wear a padded vest under my tunic, at least the stain will not be obvious."

"What do you need to wear a tunic for? I thought you only got dressed so I wouldn't see your back."

"Your handful of plums will not feed us both."

"You're joining your family for breakfast as if nothing happened?"

"I anticipate I will be cutting my food into extremely tiny pieces." Another half-smile winked briefly before fading to steely resolve. "But I will not hide in my chambers like a frightened boy. I will be the next King of Nord D'Rae and I will not allow the Queen to forget that."

Angie frowned. "The Queen? But I thought it was the King who—"

"Of course it was. Do you think for a moment I would submit myself to her judgment?" He shook his head. "No. The King wielded the lash but it was the Queen who engineered the conflict. I would not have made the mistake of directly contradicting him had she not clouded the situation with misdirection."

He stood tall with pride and righteousness, the morning sun gilding his body and reflecting a shimmering corona of light from the thick salve. At that moment, he looked less like a king-to-be and more like a young god. Remembering the epic struggles of the various Greek gods against their all-powerful father, Zeus, and how badly things had turned out for any poor humans caught in the crossfire, the image was anything but reassuring.

Reynart pulled his vest from the armoire and tossed it onto the bed. "Would you play squire for me?"

Shaking off her foolish notion, Angie picked up the vest and slipped it over his head. She let the front panel fall where it would and carefully lowered the back section so that it would not rub off any of the salve. Then she laced up the sides, binding it tightly in place.

He stretched tentatively to either side, smiling when the vest remained snug and close around his chest. "Well done, milady. I may well keep this on until arms practice this afternoon."

She gaped at him. "You're going to *fight*? Like that? What if someone hits you on the back?"

"I shall have to ensure they do not get close enough to land a blow." His eyes grew dark and his expression hardened. "There is no place for weakness on a battlefield."

"And obviously no place for sanity, either."

Chapter Seven

As Reynart left his room, he spotted the royal guard forming up before the King's door, ready to escort His Majesty downstairs. The Queen, already standing in her place, glared at him down the length of the hall. Heedless of the pain in his abused back, Reynart broke into a run and sprinted down the stone steps to the first floor.

The King's party would take the larger, formal stairs at the other end of the corridor and proceed with due ceremony and caution. They were nowhere to be seen when he rounded the last corner. Flat-out running for all he was worth, Reynart burst through the door to the morning room, startling Alaric into a futile grab for the sword he wasn't wearing.

Reynart circled around one of the tall chairs and braced his arms upon it, forcing his breathing to slow. Alaric opened his mouth to speak but fell silent as the King and Queen entered the room.

She'd hoped to trick the King into disinheriting Reynart last night and her displeasure at her continued failure to secure the heirdom for her son was evident in every stiff line of her body. She glared at Reynart, now standing properly at attention, his head bowed in acknowledgment of the King, but could find no cause for fault. The King glanced his way and smiled, an expression of his pleasure rather than an indication of any softer feelings for his elder son.

No, Your Majesty. You haven't broken me yet. This battle will continue amusing you for many years to come.

Reynart allowed none of his feelings to show on his face, although his fingers tightened their grip on the chair before him. There weren't many things he feared but the King had forced him to confront one of his deepest terrors this morning. He'd been certain that Anjeli would leave when she saw what had been done to him, especially when she'd been so distressed yesterday by the evidence of previous discipline. After all, how could he protect her if he could not protect himself?

But she hadn't reacted at all the way he feared she would. He was glad she'd accepted the situation so calmly and appreciated her help in applying the healing salve but he didn't understand why she'd done so. He knew what he wanted from her. But what did she want from him?

He said little during the meal, his attention focused on cutting the breakfast meats into pieces small enough that they did not require chewing. After watching him laboriously mincing a slice of ham that he would normally eat in four bites, the Queen snapped, "If you're going to eat your food, eat it! Don't shred it to pieces."

Surprisingly, it was the King who came to his defense. "Let him be. He has the courage to eat a man's meal, rather than calling for soup like an invalid. What does it matter how he eats it?"

Across the table from Reynart, a dull, red flush stained Alaric's face, as his brother stared pointedly at his food. Although Alaric had made nowhere near as many trips to the dungeon as his brother, he'd earned his share of discipline. The last time the King had punished him, he'd eaten nothing but soup and thin stew for three days.

Reynart counted back the years. He hadn't witnessed his brother's shame, because he'd been disowned and living in the stables, which would have placed him on the edge of fourteen and made Alaric not yet twelve. It was unfair to compare the reactions of a boy with those of a man. Not that the King had ever been concerned with being fair, but it was unusual for him to find anything good about Reynart's person or manner in the days following a disciplining.

The mystery of the King's behavior was compounded even further when, after finishing his meal, he turned to Reynart and said, "I thought upon your words last night. Did you reconsider them?"

No need to ask which words the King was talking about. Reynart fought the urge to brace for another blow and instead lowered his gaze in proper subservience.

"I was wrong to speak out of turn. I had not realized your decision had already been made. Of course, as your loyal subject, I fully support your plans to open the royal granaries and stores for a celebratory feast in the province of Caemar."

"But…?"

Reynart kept silent, although it was a trial.

"That was only a preliminary plan. I have not yet written out the orders."

He looked up, searching the King's expression for any sign of duplicity. He saw craftiness, yes, but no treachery.

Hope welled up within him. The pain in his back had kept him awake for much of the night and he'd used the time to replay the conversation with the King over and over in his mind, searching for a way that he could have made his point without contradicting the King. So he knew there was a possible compromise. The trick would be getting the King to listen with an open mind, never the easiest of tasks. And whatever he said this morning, Reynart needed to be certain that he did not insult or contradict the King in any way.

"Are you asking for my counsel, Your Majesty?"

"I would consider it."

"Then do not waste the grain on a single feast." Reynart leaned forward, the same passion that had proved his undoing last night firing him again. "The harvest season has just begun and the farmers of Caemar do not yet know how badly the summer storms damaged their crops. They may yet need those stores to survive the winter. I agree that a feast of the King's bounty will raise their spirits but let it not be at the expense of their survival."

"What would you counsel?"

Twice now the King had asked him for his opinion, and actually appeared interested in what Reynart had to say. They were in private, rather than the public setting of the hall, but that meant only that if Reynart upset him, the King would be satisfied with bellowing instead of requiring discipline. Yet if there were a chance he could still influence the King's policy, he had to take it.

Reynart pointedly folded his hands and lowered his gaze, hoping to convey that he was offering an opinion only, and not presuming to tell the King what to do. "Do not empty the stores. The people will be just as appreciative of small cakes of fine grain, especially if you sweeten them with the honey they rarely taste. Let the rest of the feast be of modest scale, relying on fresh produce and other perishables for the bulk of it."

The Queen sniffed. "So you would have the people associate the name of King Ulrich with parsimony?"

Reynart's head snapped up, as the King's confusing behavior suddenly became clear. The feast had not been his idea. He'd initially been swayed by his wife's suggestion, and so proclaimed that a feast would be held. But he had not committed himself irrevocably to any of the details of that feast. Far from making the King look weak willed or indecisive, reasoned consideration of other alternatives now would make him seem wise.

Confident of his position, Reynart turned on the Queen. "Would you rather have them cursing the King's name for allowing them to starve? Unlike you, Your Majesty, the people of Caemar will have no grasp of what a feast could entail. They will know only that they are being gifted with delicacies normally far beyond their reach, and remain unaware of the other things they could have been given but weren't."

"It is wise counsel," the King said. "I will consider it."

He stood, followed a moment later by the other three. Reynart glanced regretfully at the food he had not been able to finish, but obediently bent his head for the King's dismissal.

Instead, the King summoned the serving boy to the table. "Fill another plate for the Prince."

Then the King and Queen exited the room. Alaric and Reynart trailed behind them, the serving boy hurrying after them with the hastily filled plate. Alaric glared once at Reynart, then stiffly refused to look in his direction again as they marched up the formal stairs.

Reynart let out his breath in a sigh. Did his brother think he'd allowed himself to be dragged into the dungeons last night so that he could impress the King with his courage this morning? If so, Alaric credited him with a far more devious mind than he possessed. Unfortunately, it was not nearly as devious a plan as any of the ones the Queen was capable of brewing. No matter what the truth of the situation, Reynart suspected Alaric would shortly believe Reynart was not only trying to discredit him, he was possibly trying to overthrow the King himself.

This afternoon's sword practice would be interesting.

* * * * *

Angie and Reynart shared a companionable breakfast of bacon, ham, sausage and thumb-sized grilled medallions of meat, along with a coddled egg on cheese toast and wedges of pears. He couldn't read aloud and she didn't want to cause any additional pain by sitting in his lap, since that required her to wrap her arm around his shoulders. So after they finished eating and he put the dish outside for a servant to pick up, he sat at his desk reading, while she pulled a chair up to the window to get the best light for sewing.

Her thoughts wandered as she laboriously set each stitch in place. This was a cruel and vicious place she had landed herself in and she didn't belong here. She liked Reynart. She *really* liked Reynart. But she couldn't stay with him, hidden away and living on smuggled table scraps like some sort of secret pet. She'd been locked in these rooms for only two days but she was already getting sick of them, especially when Reynart was away. She was eager to be out and about, doing things again.

Besides, she had a family of her own to whom she needed to return. She'd successfully put off thinking about home, distracting herself with the new world in which she'd found herself. She was afraid that if she stopped to think about what she'd lost, she'd break down. Crying wouldn't solve anything and, given the mania for strength that seemed to be the norm here, might even make matters worse. But she could put off the thoughts no longer.

Her parents were probably worried sick about where she'd gone. Even if she couldn't get home right away, she wished there was a way she could let them know she was safe. No doubt they'd imagined a variety of disastrous fates for her, starting with dead-in-a-ditch and growing progressively more far-fetched and horrific. They'd never guess what had really happened, though, or be able to magically summon her home. She'd have to find a way out of here on her own. But she would find a way home. Somehow. Her absolute certainty that she would see her parents again gave her the strength to face her situation with calm reason.

She toyed with the idea of bringing Reynart back with her, once she figured out how to get home. Her mother would love him. He was good-looking and polite, her two main criteria for her daughter's potential beaux. And her father would be pleased that he was intelligent and well-educated. But she couldn't imagine Reynart giving up his princehood to be a nobody in Arizona. He'd spent too many years, and paid in too much blood, to abandon his goal of becoming King.

Gradually, she became aware of his focused gaze upon her and stopped her daydreaming. "What?"

"You are a puzzlement, milady."

"Of course I am. I'm a girl. Men have been struggling to understand the female mind for centuries."

His lips turned in a half-smile. "Then you counsel I should turn my attentions to more profitable pursuits?"

She bent her head, then looked up at him coyly through the curling wisps of hair that had already pulled free of her braids. "I didn't say that."

He gave a somewhat husky bark of laughter, as if the deep breath had pained him, and beckoned her closer. Obediently, she scooted her chair next to his.

Gently, he reached over and rested his hand upon her knee. "Then I shall keep my attention on you. Even if my attention is all I can give you at the moment."

"It will be enough." She placed her hand on top of his and squeezed lightly.

So they spent the rest of the morning sitting side by side with their own pursuits. Unless he was writing a note on his slate, Reynart was constantly in touch with Angie. Sometimes he rested his hand on her knee, while other times he caressed her thigh or stroked her arm. Even though his attention was fully on the books he was reading, he seemed to have an insatiable need to reassure himself that she was there.

At one point, tired of sewing and wanting to rest her eyes and hands, Angie captured his hand and drew it up to brush a light kiss across the back of it. He turned in surprise, then flashed her a brilliant smile, the glow only slightly diminished by the swelling and split lip.

"Any reason for that?" he asked.

"It didn't seem fair that you got to touch me and I wasn't touching you."

He nodded wisely, his stern expression diluted by the sparkle in his eyes. "You are, of course, correct. We must remedy this oversight. I would not have it said that I was unfair."

Giving up all thoughts of sewing, Angie scooted her chair closer to the desk, so that she could see the books he was reading. She stroked her fingers lightly over his thigh, caressing his solid muscle through the soft cotton of his trous. He made a soft sound of pleasure, a cross between a sigh and a growl, opening his legs and leaning back to give her easier access to his inner thigh. Then his back bumped the back of the chair.

He jerked upright with a sharp hiss, snapping his legs together.

Angie let go. Sighing, she picked up her discarded sewing, a much less dangerous way to occupy her hands. He continued to touch her and she continued to wish she could touch him without hurting him, until a servant arrived with Reynart's lunch.

As she had the day before, Angie hid in his bedroom until the servant had laid out the food and drink. She returned to see him looking at the selection with a broad grin on his face.

"You're a good man, Eomar. May the Heavenly Pair bless you and all your children."

Angie peeked around Reynart at the bowls on the table. Bits of green and white vegetables floated in a yellowish broth and what looked like a shredded version of yesterday's roast swam in a dark brown gravy. A third bowl held dark red grapes, halved and pitted.

"Are these your favorite foods?" she asked.

"No. But none of them require chewing. There's also enough here for two."

Her heart raced. "Does he know I'm here?"

"No. He knows I won't get much dinner tonight and wants to make sure I don't starve." Reynart chuckled. "He's skinny as a willow wand himself but he always makes sure all the kitchen help have plenty to eat."

"You're hardly kitchen help."

"Oh, but I was. I spent a few months as a spit boy."

"Ew, gross. You had to clean out spittoons?"

Reynart laughed. "No, milady. A spit boy stands next to the fire and turns the spit. It requires constant attention. Turn the spit too fast and the meat doesn't cook. Too slow, and the meat burns. Eomar showed me how to wait for the juices to start bubbling out, then turn it just fast enough for the juices to run along the surface."

Angie smiled, pleased to share what was obviously a happy memory for him. She could hear a lingering sense of pride in his voice and could just imagine him as a young boy, thrilled with his mastery of the difficult task.

"How old were you?"

"Four or five."

"What? And they let you stand next to an open fire? Working?"

Reynart looked quizzically at her. "What else was I supposed to do? I had to eat. And if I wanted to do that, I had to work."

"But you're a prince."

"Not then I wasn't. That was the first time the King reversed his decision of paternity and declared I wasn't his son after all. I was summarily dispatched from the castle."

His mouth pursed, as if the memory still tasted bitter. "I was too young to understand what they were talking about, of course. The castle was the only home I'd known, so I snuck back in as people came in for dinner. I was clever enough to avoid the hall where the King and Queen would be but, since I was hungry, I went down to the kitchens. Eomar tried to chase me off but, once I explained what had happened, he found a way for me to be useful. Ladria discovered me there and convinced me to stay in the kitchens until it was safe for me to return to the nursery suite."

Angie stared at him in horror. His father had disowned him and thrown him out of his home with no consideration for how he would eat or where he would sleep, when Reynart was barely more than a toddler. Having been thoroughly fussed over her entire life, she couldn't imagine a father ever treating his child that way. Although she supposed she should expect as much from a man who would whip his son just for disagreeing with him.

"You stayed in the kitchens as a spit boy for months?" she finally asked.

"A little over one month that first time." His eyes took on a distant look, as he tried to recall more details. "I went back…seven times in all. Sometimes for less than a week. The longest was three months. Usually it was for about two weeks."

"And you were always a spit boy?"

"Yes. Of course, once I got older, I couldn't hide in the kitchens any longer. The older boys are expected to serve at the tables."

"Where did you hide then?"

"The stables, at first. I was willing to share a stall with my horse, since his temper kept everyone else away. And once the stable hands realized I was willing to help clean the stalls, they let me stay."

"You said at first. You stayed someplace else, afterwards?"

"The last time, when I was fourteen, I presented myself to the captain of the guard. By law, anyone who passes a series of basic tests must be admitted for training. I knew enough swordsmanship to pass the tests, although he tried to make me fail. He faced me against one of the most experienced members of the guard to test my skills and ordered that we fight in real time rather than at practice speed." He bared his teeth in a savage grin that had nothing in common with his earlier lighthearted expression. "I won."

"You beat an experienced swordsman? Were you that good?"

He shook his head. "In skill with a sword? No. But that's not what determines who wins a fight. He started slow, feeling me out, so I fought poorly at first. Then, when he thought he knew my strengths and weaknesses, I was able to surprise him."

Angie laughed. "I bet there were some real fireworks the first time you turned out with the guards on the practice field."

"Yes. I was through with hiding and the King must have received fifteen reports of my activities within the first candlemark. He declared my martial abilities were proof that I was his son after all and I went back to being a prince." He shrugged, no longer wincing at the motion. "And I've been a prince ever since."

* * * * *

They shared lunch and Reynart listened eagerly to Anjeli's stories of her childhood. Her world was a strange and unusual place, although he could tell she was trying to frame her explanations in terms he would understand. So he nodded sagely at her descriptions of dancing lessons and competing on a swimming team. At one point, she seemed to say that young girls were all transformed into bluebirds so that they could learn skills that would make them good chatelaines, which seemed an odd method of training. Her clarification was not much better, having to do with the mysterious rites of young women, although he did grasp that she had not ever actually been a bird.

Despite all the oddities of her world, however, the two things he found most fascinating about her childhood were that she was an only child and she had a mother and father who adored her.

Ladria had always been a devoted sister to him, almost a surrogate mother at times for all she was not even a year older, and his staunchest defender after she came into her mage powers. And so much of his life had been shaped by his competition with Alaric to be heir to the throne.

He could not imagine what it would be like to grow up with neither. And while intellectually, he knew there must be parents somewhere who loved their children without restraint, he had never seen any in the court. He had to fight the urge to keep asking her if she was perhaps exaggerating or misinterpreting her parents' motives.

He could have listened to her talk about her world for hours but the chiming of the *Novem* bells recalled him to duty. Taking his leave, he hurried down to the practice field.

Mastersmith Gage was waiting for him at the entrance to the field.

"My lord Prince, I have finished your knives." The smith smiled, the pride of a master craftsman evident in the way he presented the case for Reynart's approval.

Reynart opened the case. Nestled inside on a velvet background lay the six knives he had commissioned. Unlike ordinary steel knives, these had blades of black volcanic glass, honed to razor sharpness on each of the tiny serrations along their sides, then tempered with magic until they were as hard as diamond. The handles were not steel or wood, but silver, delicately wrought to encase the glass blade.

He lifted one out of the case and balanced it on his finger. It wavered for a moment, then held level. "Perfect," he breathed.

The smith bowed, accepting Reynart's praise. "The design was a worthy challenge."

Reynart pulled back the sleeve of his practice tunic and replaced the two knives in his left vambrace with two of the new ones. He flexed his arm, triggering the release mechanism. The glass knife slid smoothly into his hand, the silver hilt perfectly positioned to throw the blade.

He returned the knife to its sheath. "Mastersmith, you have outdone yourself."

Reynart would have loved to stay and practice with his new knives but the students were forming into lines to prepare for the advent of the weaponsmaster and he needed to take his place. He nodded once more to the mastersmith, then took his sword and crossed the field to stand beside Alaric.

"Are you able to fight?" Alaric whispered softly.

"I don't have a choice, do I?" Reynart murmured in reply, his eyes focused forward so that the weaponsmaster would not see them talking in line when he arrived. But his heart was warmed by his brother's obvious concern. Despite all the Queen's efforts to drive a wedge between them, when Reynart needed him, Alaric would still be there for him. Fifteen years of brotherhood could not be so easily destroyed.

"We could ask the weaponsmaster to focus on forms today."

"No. If he thinks I'm showing weakness, he'll do all the drills requiring dropping and rolling on the ground, just to teach me a lesson. I'm safer in mock battles."

Weaponsmaster Tyson strode onto the practice field, glaring at the assembled students as if they were the worst excuses for fighters he'd ever seen. Since he'd been glaring at them all for years in the same way, they ignored his sour expression.

"Form up, groups of two, end of line to beginning of line."

The two-dozen students paired off as instructed. Reynart faced Olivier, the son of a hill country baron. Olivier traced his ancestry through seven generations of nobility, first hill country chieftains, then after their annexation by Reynart's grandfather, barons of Nord D'Rae. He'd disliked Reynart for his common heritage since they'd been boys together.

"And here I thought your face couldn't get any uglier," Olivier sneered, raising his sword. "The whole castle knows you were whipped like a disobedient dog last night."

Reynart silently lifted his sword to guard position.

The weaponsmaster walked through the pairings, checking his students' positions. "Today we will work on battlefield maneuvering. Fight your opponent without getting in the way of your neighbors' fights."

Reynart glanced at Alaric, who faced Darvell. Smaller than the prince and faster on his feet, Darvell would either win their bout quickly or be worn down beneath Alaric's greater power and endurance. Reynart suspected half the times Darvell let Alaric win, simply to end their matches, once he'd determined he wasn't going to have an easy victory. If Darvell controlled the fight, he'd force Alaric to chase him up and down the field and could get in the way of many of the other matches.

The pair on his other side were unimaginative nobles who would face each other square-on and trade blows until one fell. Nothing to worry about from them.

"Begin!"

Reynart's attention was focused entirely on Olivier as the noble attacked with a flurry of slashing blows. Reynart blocked blow after blow as they circled each other, deflecting the force of the attacks using the strength of his arm. He heard the ringing of steel on steel and the other students' grunts of effort as a collage of sound important only as an indication of their positions relative to himself.

"What's the matter?" Olivier taunted. "Can't swing your sword today?"

Eventually, Reynart saw the opening he was looking for, dodging a wild blow and coming in tight with a full stroke that burned like fire across the muscles of his back.

Olivier managed to deflect the blow and the follow-up, although the blade nicked his shoulder before he pushed it away.

"Looks like I can," Reynart answered.

Hatred burned in Olivier's eyes. "The weaponsmaster said battlefield conditions. Prepare to die, Prince."

"Not by your sword."

Bellowing a hill country war cry, Olivier charged. Reynart blocked the blows but every one ripped across his shoulders until he could hear and see nothing but the nobleman before him and the sword coming for his blood. Twice Olivier overextended and left himself open for a counterattack but Reynart couldn't bring his sword around with enough force to reach him.

Their swords locked together, each struggling to bind the other and force a break in his defenses. Olivier's gaze darted over Reynart's shoulder and a wave of sound crashed into his senses as he tried to identify if there was a real threat behind him or if Olivier was trying to trick him. Booted feet hit the ground in cadence, running directly at him.

Abandoning the battle for the swords, Reynart twisted, dropping to one knee. A knife was in his hand, then flying at the attacker before he even registered him as Darvell, sword raised and face twisted in fury. His expression shifted to shock as he looked down at the silver hilt protruding from his chest.

"Hold!" the weaponsmaster bellowed. "Mage!"

The army mage waiting on the sidelines raced to Darvell's side to heal the injury before it could kill the nobleman. The need for the weapon that caused the injury was not a problem, since the mage had to pull the blade out of the nobleman's chest in order to heal him.

Secure that the immediate threat had been neutralized, Reynart checked quickly for any other potential threats, then searched the field for his brother. Alaric was just climbing to his feet from where Darvell had laid him out before beginning his charge toward Reynart.

The army mage began the healing, focusing all eyes on Darvell. He lay on the ground, screaming from the pain of accelerated healing, until he blacked out.

Meanwhile, Reynart scanned the faces of the other students, looking for anyone who might have been privy to Darvell's plans. He would have expected such an attack from Olivier, or even one of the handfuls of other nobles who took every opportunity to try to make him look bad in front of the weaponsmaster. But he'd never had any quarrel with Darvell. Someone had bribed him, with money or the promise of power, to try and assassinate Reynart.

His first suspicion fell on the Queen. As Alaric's sixteenth birthday approached, she was growing increasingly desperate. Had she finally decided she couldn't get Reynart out of the way by disinheriting him and that she would have to kill him? It was the most likely explanation, but not the only one.

There were courtiers who would prefer to see Alaric on the throne because he could be more easily manipulated. And Reynart could not discount the possibility of revenge for any of the men he had killed in this summer's war, the men under his command who had died or even some real or imagined situation he was ignorant of for which someone held him responsible. But until any other members of this conspiracy revealed themselves, he would assume it was the Queen's doing.

The other students had gathered around in a silent circle, not sure what had happened and waiting to see what would happen next. Glancing curiously at the glass blade, the mage handed the knife, hilt-first, to the weaponsmaster before turning his attention back to his patient. Weaponsmaster Tyson flipped the knife in his hand, admiring the design and balance, then handed it to Reynart. He cleaned the blade and slid the knife back into his vambrace.

"We were not training with knives today," the weaponsmaster said quietly, almost conversationally.

"We were training in battlefield conditions. All weapons are allowed in battle."

"So they are. Your aim was slightly to the left of true."

"I didn't have time to aim. I turned to see him charging at me with his sword raised and reacted to the threat."

"Do you know why he was attacking you instead of his partner?"

"No. Given the circumstances, I didn't think the reason was important."

But he would find out as soon as Darvell was left unguarded so that Reynart could obtain truthful answers from him. The danger surrounding Reynart was rapidly escalating, which placed Anjeli in additional peril as well. If he did not trust her so completely, he might think she'd been sent specifically to distract him at this time when he needed all his wits about him. Instead, the need to protect her life as well as his own only increased his vigilance.

The weaponsmaster turned away to address the rest of his students, except Darvell, who was being dragged away by the mage. Alaric had rejoined the group, although he kept darting nervous glances toward his brother. Reynart tried to smile and indicate he was fine but, judging from Alaric's pasty expression, he'd revealed more of his inner turmoil than he'd intended.

"The practice field is for the study of the arts of war. If you cannot leave your personal grudges or petty disagreements behind you, you will end up injured, like Darvell, or in a real fight, dead. There are no mages on hand to clean up your mistakes during a war. Everyone except Prince Reynart, form into pairs again. When I give the signal, you will begin fighting. But I want you to remain aware of the other fighters around you. Especially ones without an opponent. In a real battle, they might turn and attack you."

The weaponsmaster glanced at Reynart, a smile of unholy glee lighting his features. "Get wooden practice daggers from the stores. Then walk around the practice field and throw them at whomever you feel is not sufficiently aware of possible threats."

Reynart nodded and went to do the weaponsmaster's bidding. He understood Tyson's unspoken lesson, as well. If he knew of anyone else who might hold a grudge against him, he was free to attack and make the noblemen think twice about acting upon their disputes in Tyson's class.

* * * * *

Angie woke from her brief nap when Reynart returned from dinner, carrying a basket of food. He grinned as she stopped in the doorway and stared at the bounty.

"Eomar had it all prepared. One of the servers gave it to me as the high table was leaving."

She was touched by the cook's concern. It was nice to know that someone here cared about Reynart.

The basket was packed with the same foods that had been served that night but Eomar had minced them all into tiny pieces. There was enough food for both of them to eat their fill and still have some left over for her breakfast tomorrow.

But he had disturbing news for her, as well. "The maid, Katya, was killed today."

Angie pictured the girl's terrified expression when she'd seen them on the steps. At the time, she'd seemed to be overreacting. But she'd been right to be afraid. "How?"

"One of the guards apparently realized she knew something and was questioning her. He hit her too hard. Fortunately, she died before she could betray you."

"How can you say that so calmly? A girl was *killed!*"

His face took on a stony cast. "Servants die. Even children of nobility can be taken to the very boundaries of Amin-Ra's realm. That is just how life is. The weaker are at the mercy of the stronger. I may be able to change some of that when I am King but I can do nothing now."

Angie swallowed, horrified as much by what he was saying as by what had happened. She knew him well enough by now to know he would never accept a platitude like "that's how life is" unless he had thoroughly tested it. At some point in his life, he had tried to protect a servant and failed. She suspected that failure had led to the beating he'd alluded to on her first day here, the one that nearly killed him.

"I hate your world," she said at last. "I can hardly wait to be back in my own world, where I'm safe and no one is killing people to try and find me."

"Ladria will know what to do when she returns. If you wish to return to your own world, I am certain that she will find a way to do so. But until then, know that I will protect you and keep you safe, milady."

He looked so fierce, she couldn't help but feel better. What did it matter that the entire castle guard was looking for her? Reynart had defeated the best of the guardsmen when he was only fourteen. If he thought he could take on the entire guard now to keep her safe, she'd believe him. She wouldn't allow herself to think otherwise.

They returned to their meal and soon the maid's fate and Angie's danger were put behind them, as they ate, laughed and traded lingering caresses disguised as reaching for more food.

When they had finished, Reynart asked hesitantly, "Would you apply another dose of the salve?"

"Of course!"

He walked over to the shelves but, when he returned, he was holding two jars, the familiar blue and gold jar and also a small red one.

"Is that another salve?"

"No. A powder." He opened the red jar and used the tiny spoon inside it to measure a helping of pale green powder into her half-finished tea, then swirled the tea until the powder dissolved and handed it to her. "Drink up."

"What is it?"

"I borrowed it from my sister. It prevents pregnancies."

Angie clutched the tea glass, her heart leaping. "Does that mean you're feeling well enough? After this afternoon, I was afraid…"

Reynart laughed. "I intend for you to be on your back, not for me to be on mine."

She grinned, then swallowed the now bitter tea in one long gulp. Soon, they were in the bedroom and he was presenting his naked back for her ministrations.

The swelling was almost completely gone, with just a slight puffiness where the knots had been. But his skin had turned an alarming yellow-green.

"Is it supposed to be that color?"

"What color?"

She tried to think of something he'd be familiar with to compare it to. "Very much like the chicken soup we had for lunch, but a bit more green."

"That's fine. It's just a bruise healing. Red or purple are the colors you don't want to see."

She inspected his back thoroughly, but saw no sign of any red or purple skin. Holding her breath, she opened the jar of salve, then smeared it on the bruises. He didn't wince or pull away as he had that morning, so it must be feeling better in addition to looking better.

Finished applying the salve, her hands continued stroking down his back, to the base of his spine, then the firm muscles of his ass.

"Put the cover on the jar of salve," he said.

His lack of interest in her caresses was like a cold wind through the open window, snapping her out of her dreamy haze. She covered the jar and leaned forward to set it on the bedstand.

Reynart grabbed her and pulled her around in front of him, his rampant cock tucked between them. He undid her belt, then tugged his old tunic and her chemise over her head, so that she was as naked as he. Then he was kissing her, his lips still vaguely menthol-flavored from the salve, as he stroked and caressed her back, crushing her breasts against his chest.

She reached out to hug him as well, then thought better of touching his back. Needing to hold and caress him, she put her hands on his ass, pulling his hips closer and kneading the solid muscles.

Those muscles flexed beneath her fingers as he rocked his hips, rubbing his cock against her stomach.

Then he was walking, pushing her backwards until her legs bumped the side of the bed. She climbed on, her hips sinking into the soft down of the comforter, and lay back with her legs spread. Warm moisture was already collecting between her legs, ready to ease his passage, and she trembled, eager to have him once again filling her and moving deep inside her. The moisture became a deep pool.

Reynart followed her onto the bed, kneeling between her open legs. Gently, he stroked her damp skin, probing her folds with his fingers. Two fingers slid over the edge of her portcullis and she moaned in pleasure, her hips rising to take him deeper. He stroked and teased, circling the entrance and pressing against her as he slicked his fingers back and forth across her gateway. Moaning and writhing, she begged incoherently for more. Then he twisted his hand, so that he could flick his thumb across her barbican.

She stuffed a corner of the coverlet into her mouth to muffle her scream as the pleasure claimed her, arching her back and clenching around his fingers until all her muscles went slack and she collapsed into the soft comforter. Before she could completely gather her wits, she realized his fingers were still stroking her, inflaming her quivering flesh.

When he took his hand away, she whimpered softly. But his fingers were replaced almost immediately by the head of his cock, nudging her portcullis wide open.

She gasped, tensing with remembered pain. Then he was kissing her, his lips gentle but insistent as he nibbled along her jaw line. He worked his way up the length of her jaw, then licked and suckled her earlobe.

"Welcome me into your keep, Anjeli," he whispered, his hot breath steaming her ear.

Closing her eyes, she lifted her hips and felt his cock slide deep inside her. They sighed in unison.

"Why me?" she whispered, needing to know that he was making love to her and not just to the first woman to show him any kindness.

"You are beautiful." His cock slid out, then thrust deep again. "Kind."

She sighed in pleasure and he continued stroking in and out with each word.

"Gentle. Funny. Giving. Innocent. You make me happy…just to be with you. And I want…to make you…as happy…to be with me."

Then he was moving too fast for words, pumping into her as he grunted and gasped, and she reached blindly for the bliss that was just out of reach. Clutching his ass, she urged him to move even faster, stroking deeper. His breath rasped in shallow pants, a rumbling growl deep in his chest gaining in pitch and volume until he grabbed her by the shoulders, pinning her to the bed, and arched backward, driving deep inside her. He held the pose for a long moment, trembling, then loosed a hoarse gasp as he filled her with the rush of his release. He collapsed limply on top of her, his shaking arms barely able to support his weight so that he didn't crush her.

She whimpered, still searching for the bliss that had been denied her, and he shifted position enough to reach between their bodies and fondle her barbican until she shuddered and cried out, collapsing spent beneath him.

They lay together in silence, their breathing gradually slowing, their heart rates returning to normal. He pushed at the covers until they were between the sheets instead of on top of them, then pulled the comforter up and curled on his side beside her, one hand idly stroking her ribs, stomach and breasts.

"Why you?" he whispered. "Because you not only welcome me to your bed, you welcome my thoughts and conversation when we are out of it. You share not only your body, but your heart and mind. How could I not want you?"

"I think I love you."

Her declaration was met by silence, even his hand freezing its restless motion. She turned to face him, terrified that she had frightened him away by mentioning love too quickly, and that he was even now trying to think of a way to escape from her snare.

Instead, his face was a picture of stunned disbelief. He blinked, then blinked again and swallowed.

"I am honored, milady. And I shall endeavor to be worthy of such a gift."

Smiling, she closed her eyes and snuggled up against him, feeling his strong arms wrap around her to hold her close through the night. It was all right if he didn't say he loved her in return. He'd had little enough experience of the emotion and probably couldn't recognize it. But she could feel the truth in his actions and in the other things he said. He loved her. She was certain of it.

She couldn't see how they could possibly have a future together but that was unimportant. If they truly loved each other, they would find a way. Somehow. After all, she'd been magically transported to another world just to be with him. That must mean they were meant to be together.

Chapter Eight

Their days fell into a comfortable pattern. Reynart read and made notes while Angie sewed or listened to him talk, then they shared lunch. Afterward, they would tell each other stories of their lives, talking about anything and everything, and end up making love until he had to leave for his weapons practice. The memory of the poor, terrified maid, killed in the hunt for Angie, convinced her to stay inside the two rapidly shrinking rooms, although she often looked longingly out of the narrow arrow-slit windows when she was alone. So she sewed and, when she tired of sewing, tried to puzzle out some of Reynart's books until he returned. She'd help him dress for dinner, then nap until he arrived with food for her. He'd undress while she ate, then they'd go to bed, making love until they were exhausted and finally succumbed to sleep.

So Angie was surprised when she woke to find the bed beside her empty.

"Reynart?" she called softly.

Silence answered her and she realized she'd been hearing a faint scratching sound from the other room that had now stopped. A moment later, Reynart appeared in the doorway. He was already dressed.

"I'm copying out my analysis for the King."

"That's right. You said last night you thought you'd finished it but you wanted to sleep on it to be sure."

"I was correct. It was finished."

She smiled, stretching under the covers. "So what were you planning to do this morning, since you no longer have to read?"

Desire flared in his eyes and he took a deep breath. "I like your idea of how to spend the morning. But it is not safe."

"What do you mean? Does that powder of your sister's lose its effectiveness?"

He shook his head. "Not physically unsafe. Politically. The only reason no one has questioned how much time I've spent in my rooms is because they know I've been working on this analysis for the King. Now I need to be seen. First, so it's obvious I am confident in my work and do not need to be rushing up until the moment of our meeting. And second, so that no one suspects I have any other reason to be here. Remember what happened to Katya."

Angie shuddered.

"You're right. I don't like it but it's the smart thing to do." She sat up, revising her vision of a leisurely morning in bed with him to a morning spent alone with the stupid sewing or the books she was too stupid to understand. Neither alternative was the least bit appealing. Trying to keep the envy from her voice, she asked, "What will you be doing?"

"I thought I'd go for a ride. They let my horse out in the paddock, of course, but it's not the same. He needs a good run."

She sighed. "I never thought I'd be jealous of a horse. But I'd love to get out and run, too. Or just get out and stand in the sunshine with the wind blowing in my face.

I'd even be happy to stand in the pouring rain, so long as I was outside."

Reynart came over and sat beside her on the bed. Putting his arm around her shoulders, he cuddled her close, tucking her cheek against his chest and nuzzling her hair. The tension and frustration that had been building in her dissolved beneath his gentle touch and she snuggled closer, putting her arms loosely around his healed back.

"You will not need to hide forever, Anjeli. My sister will be home any day now. Her last message said she might arrive as soon as yesterday, but no later than midweek next. I'm hoping she will be able to protect you from Gervaise by passing you off as her new maid, so you can stay in the castle. But if that won't work, she'll be able to use her magic to disguise you long enough for us to smuggle you out of the castle to someplace in the city where you would be safe."

Angie kissed the vee of warm skin showing through the neck of his tunic. His arms tightened around her as his breath escaped on a soft groan.

"Ah, Anjeli. How can I protect you when your lightest touch makes me forget everything except what it feels like to be sheathed inside you?"

She followed the path of her kiss with her tongue, tasting his spice-scented skin. He groaned again, his head tipping back to allow her free access to the tender skin of his throat.

"I didn't hear the come-to-breakfast bells yet."

"No. I woke early. To finish my copies."

"Did you finish them?"

"Yes. One for the King and one for me."

Angie twisted her body, falling back down onto the bed and pulling Reynart on top of her. "Then there's plenty of time."

He lifted himself off of her just enough to unfasten his trous and push them out of the way. His cock was already swollen with desire, tenting the bottom of his tunic. Angie bunched the fabric at his waist, freeing him. The sight of his long, hard cock made her mouth dry and her channel wet.

Taking the tunic from her, he pulled it the rest of the way over his head and tossed it aside. Then he was positioning himself between her legs, the head of his cock lifting to her portcullis. She gasped, not quite ready, but opening immediately at his welcome touch.

He stilled. "Did I—?"

Grabbing his firm ass with both hands, she lifted her hips as she pulled him down, sheathing him fully in her body. His question faded into a groan of pleasure.

Then he was sliding slowly in and out of her, kissing and licking her chest, breasts and neck as he moved. She kneaded the flexing muscles of his ass, urging him to move faster, but he continued his teasing tempo.

"You were the one who said we had plenty of time," he reminded her, pressing kisses along her jaw.

She slid her hands up over his hips to his back. His skin was smooth and supple, with no signs of the beating he'd endured earlier in the week. As her fingers stroked along his spine, he sighed, arching into her touch.

Slowly, Angie rolled her caresses up his spine. When she reached the balance point somewhere around his shoulder blades, Reynart stopped trying to arch backwards into her touch and instead slumped forward, pressing the length of his body against hers. He mumbled incoherent sounds of pleasure into her neck, followed by a plaintive noise of protest when she stopped. But she'd had all week to find out what pleased him and so confidently placed her thumbs on either side of his spine and stroked all the way to the base, arching her body beneath his as she did so.

His reaction was instantaneous, his cock swelling within her.

He began kissing and nibbling her skin in a frenzied effort to taste as much of her as possible, while he held her tipped hips and slicked his cock in and out at an equally frantic pace.

Her breath escaped in gasped cries of pleasure as she clutched him tightly and her body begged for release. She trembled, whimpering, and he stroked even faster, thrusting hard and deep. With every thrust, her breath caught in hopeful wonderment. Would this be the one? Together, they paused, before he pulled out to thrust again with a hoarse grunt.

He thrust again, his cock fully embedded deep within her. A strangled sound escaped him and he arched his back, pressing himself even further into her. His arms trembled with the strain and she rocked her hips urgently.

"Not yet. Not yet. Not yet," she begged.

"I can't wait," he gasped. But he braced his weight on one arm and reached between their sweating bodies with the other, finding her swollen barbican and squeezing it.

Angie succumbed to the ecstasy, waves of pleasure rippling through her. The waves squeezed his cock and then Reynart cried out, filling her with the hot spurt of his release. He collapsed, shuddering, on top of her, rolling them to their sides so that he didn't crush her. Together they clung to each other, riding out the ripples of their lovemaking, his spent cock still twitching within her and boosting her heightened senses over the edge again.

As their breathing softened and their pulses slowed, the distant chime of bells drifted through the window.

Reynart chuckled softly and kissed her temple. "You were right. Plenty of time. But now I have to go. I'll try to bring back enough food to hold you through to dinner, since I will not be here to receive a luncheon."

She smiled, stretching languidly and admiring his beautiful face through half-closed eyes. "Don't worry. I won't be hungry. You've tired me out enough to sleep straight through until this afternoon."

* * * * *

Despite her assurances to the contrary, Angie was up well before noon and eagerly devouring the fruit and cheese Reynart had left for her. When the doorknob rattled, she thought he'd returned early from his ride. Until she heard a man's muffled exclamation of pain on the other side of the door.

The knob turned and the door opened a crack, just enough to allow an unknown hand to reach inside, feeling up and down the door for the trigger to the crossbow. He found the hook to which the line was usually attached, although Reynart had left it disabled so that she would not stumble against the string.

The hand disappeared and a man said, "He didn't arm it before he left. He's getting careless. Are the magical wards still in place?"

"Yes, my lord Prince. You felt the reminder when you touched the knob," a second man answered.

"Then cancel them. Quickly. The guard has agreed to turn the other way but that won't help if anyone else sees us."

One of the jars on the shelf began glowing, so brightly that she could not look at it. Then her slow-moving wits finally threw themselves into high gear. Reynart's brother and a mage, probably Gervaise, were breaking into Reynart's rooms. She had no idea what they were looking for but they clearly expected the rooms to be empty. They couldn't find her here!

Grabbing the remains of her breakfast from the table, she hurried into the bedroom and hid in the armoire, wedging herself into the taller side and pressing her ear to the crack in the door to hear what was going on outside.

A crash of shattering pottery and glass announced the end of whatever magical wards Reynart used to guard his door. Footsteps hurried into the room, followed by the outer door shutting.

"Now, where would he put his analysis for the King? If I can find out how he is planning to arrange the rebels, I can defeat them from my towers. The King will be so impressed with my grasp of strategy, he will put me in charge of commanding the tower defenses. And I will prove my bravery to him once and for all. He'll name me his heir and everything will finally be as it should be."

"As you say, my lord Prince."

"Don't just stand there! Help me look. After all, if your magic had worked, I wouldn't need to be doing this."

"It did work. The magic was summoned…" His voice faded, then he snapped, "The magic is here."

Alaric snorted. "Of course it is. Ladria gives all her enchanted trinkets to Reynart because no one else will have them. The shelves are full of magical bric-a-brac."

"Be quiet. I'm thinking."

A crash sounded, as if the desk or table had been overturned. "Don't you talk to me like that! I'm going to be your next King! I give the orders, not you. You do as I say."

"Yes, my lord Prince. Of course. Forgive me." The mage's apology was patently insincere, bordering on outright mockery, but Alaric apparently only heard the words, not the tone in which they were delivered.

"That's better. Now, stop wasting time and help me find Reynart's plans."

"I will look in the other room."

The mage entered the bedroom, muttering to himself. "Insufferable codswollop. You really think I would waste the last three years creating a spell with no better purpose than making you King? If I didn't need your blood to control the magic, you'd die with everyone else."

Angie stuffed her fist in her mouth, to stifle her involuntary gasp. They were planning on killing the King and Reynart, as well as an indeterminate number of other people, so Alaric could become King. She didn't care about the King. He deserved it for what he'd done to Reynart through the years. But she'd heard the love in Reynart's voice when he talked about his younger brother. For Alaric to repay that love with attempted murder was despicable. Worse than despicable. Reprehensible! Her vocabulary failed her and she couldn't think of any description worse than reprehensible. But whatever it was, Alaric was it.

"The magic is stronger in here," Gervaise murmured. "Not bound to an object. But harnessed, not wild. Waiting to be tapped."

Angie shifted position slightly and put her eye to the crack in the armoire. She expected the mage to be some elderly Merlin type, in long black robes and a pointy hat. Instead, he was a fat, middle-aged man in red velvet trous and overtunic, with a yellow silk undertunic that matched the hose covering his bloated legs. Spidery embellishments of gold embroidery decorated the overtunic and completely covered his ridiculous red velvet slippers.

He was staring at the rumpled bed.

Then he turned, looking straight at the armoire. Angie cringed backward, trying to pull some tunics in front of her to hide behind. Silently, she prayed, "Don't open the door. Don't open the door."

He opened the door.

They stared at each other for a moment, then he grabbed her by the braids and hauled her out of the armoire. She stumbled as she fell out.

"Let go of me!"

Alaric ran into the bedroom, stopping in the doorway and staring. "Who's she?"

"I told you the spell worked! This is our visitor. Prince Reynart has been hiding her."

Angie looked at the prince, amazed at how little he resembled his brother. If she hadn't known who he was, she'd never have guessed from seeing him. He was younger than her, obviously still a growing teenager and a good four inches shorter than Reynart, although he was already thicker. It looked like muscle, now, although she expected in a few years he'd run to fat. And he had dark blond hair and blue eyes instead of Reynart's black hair and green eyes. But the biggest difference was his expression. Where Reynart's eyes held quiet intelligence, Alaric's had the fixed stubbornness of a mule.

His gaze dropped to her legs and a sly smile twisted his lips. "She's wearing one of his old tunics. Do you think she arrived naked? Maybe she needs to be naked again in order to release the magic."

It was useless to struggle against both men, especially since, even if she managed to elude them and escape the room, there was no place for her to go. So she fell back on the only defense she had left. Attitude.

Lifting her chin and squaring her shoulders, she said in her most haughty voice, "I'll have you know I arrived fully clothed in a proper gown. I merely find a shirtdress to be more comfortable. I was not anticipating guests."

Alaric blinked, looking a bit like a large bull that had just blundered into an electric fence.

Gervaise muttered something under his breath and Angie's arms glued themselves to her sides.

"What did you—?"

Her question was cut off, as her voice left her. Her mouth continued moving but no sound emerged. She started screaming at the top of her lungs. Silently.

Reynart had tired to warn her about the mage but she hadn't understood. The violence of swords and fists was a familiar danger, and one whose effects she could easily imagine. She'd associated magic with the flashy tricks of stage magicians, impressive but insubstantial. But in this world, magic was just as real as swords or daggers. Worse, you couldn't see it coming or block its effect.

She turned to face Gervaise, now recognizing him as the bigger threat. He'd used magic against her, trapping her somehow. There was no way she could run from them now. She could not even voice a protest.

She'd been frightened when Reynart had pulled his dagger on her. But she'd known he wouldn't use it unless she gave him a reason to distrust her. Her fear had stemmed from not knowing what he might consider a reason, since she didn't understand the rules of the world in which she'd found herself.

Now, she was terrified.

"We will take her to my rooms," Gervaise announced, throwing one of Reynart's cloaks around her shoulders to hide her attire. "The spell can be completed there."

Spell? What spell? Bits and pieces of their conversation skittered and bounced in her brain, forming connections, breaking apart and forming new connections. With an almost physical snap, the pieces fell into place.

Gervaise had cast a magical spell to summon her. The first part of the spell had succeeded, since she was here. But he'd summoned her for a reason. He needed her somehow for him to perform the big spell that he was planning. The spell that would kill the King and Reynart. There must be something she could do to stop him!

She tried to lock her legs, refusing to move. Gervaise casually slapped her face.

"Don't be a fool. You will accompany us. Prince Alaric will be happy to encourage you if you fail to move."

She glanced past the mage to the young prince, standing in the doorway. He was eyeing her with a hungry gaze, his fingers flexing as he licked his lips. Oddly, it wasn't a sexual hunger, or at least, not mostly.

She felt instead like a trophy, a possession that was coveted because it belonged to Reynart, and Alaric passionately wanted anything that was Reynart's for himself.

He didn't hate his brother, she realized. He wanted to *be* his brother. Reynart had told her about Alaric's youthful hero worship of him, the big brother who defeated a full member of the guard in a sword fight, who broke the stallion the horse trainers had abandoned as untrainable and who dared to stand up to the King, arguing his cases so persuasively, he convinced the King more often than not.

This whole mess could be solved. If she could just talk to him, she was certain she could make Alaric see reason. He didn't really want Reynart dead.

She started to say so, then remembered the magic that was keeping her silent. A frustrated, yet soundless, profanity left her lips. Sooner or later they'd release the spell holding her mute or it would wear off. She'd just have to talk quickly when she got the chance.

With Gervaise in front of her and Alaric behind her, they walked into the main room. The crash she'd heard earlier had been the table and one of the chairs overturning.

Behind her, Alaric paused. "Should we right the furniture?"

"Why? Prince Reynart will know someone has been here when he sees his wards are broken and his guest is missing."

Alaric sucked in a sharp breath. "The morning after you cast your spell, he asked me if you'd found your missing girl. But she was here in his rooms the whole time.

He knew we were up to something and was digging for more information. It's much too risky—"

Gervaise spun around, glaring at the young prince. "What would you do instead? Leave the girl, who now knows too much? We must proceed."

"Yes, of course. You're correct." He took a shaky breath. "Reynart will not return from his ride until a candlemark before *Novem*. Even if he suspects us, he will be too late to stop us."

"Then let us hurry and ensure he does not gain the opportunity."

Angie tried once again to lock her legs and refuse to move forward. Alaric punched her in the back, driving her forward to crash against Gervaise. Unable to use her hands to catch herself, she bit the thick velvet of his overtunic to keep from falling flat on her face. The mage staggered under her sudden weight, then set her back on her feet and glared at the prince.

"A modicum of restraint might be in order, my lord Prince."

Alaric shrugged. "She's moving, isn't she?"

Reluctantly, Angie followed Gervaise out of the room. She could not run away, not with her arms glued to her sides and no sense of balance. If she resisted, she might gain a few minutes, but Reynart would not be back for hours. It would not be enough of a delay. A better option would be to let them think she was cooperating and then try to mess up Gervaise's spell when they weren't paying as close attention to her.

Their strange little parade marched down the hall. Angie shuddered as they turned past the stairwell where she and Reynart had encountered Katya. But they continued on, entering the first room in the next corridor. The mage's sitting room was cramped and cluttered, with books stacked on the shelves and spilling across the table. The library-like feel was enhanced by the spiral staircase of wrought iron in the back corner of the room.

"Take her upstairs," Gervaise ordered. "I will gather the items I need."

Angie balked at the stairs. They were too small, barely an inch wide at the center and no more than four inches at the edge. She might have ventured up them if she'd had the use of her hands and could clutch a banister but her hands were frozen and there was no banister. Alaric sensed her hesitation.

"Up the stairs. Or I'll carry you up."

To be in his arms while he ascended without free hands for balance was even worse than her climbing the stairs! Consoling herself that, if she fell, at least she'd take Alaric with her, Angie put her foot on the first tread. Carefully, she lifted her other foot to the next step. Alaric followed her, one hand loosely wrapped around the center post for balance.

She considered leaning backward and sending them both crashing down the stairs. But she couldn't be certain that would stop him and Gervaise from performing their spell. And the odds were too high that she'd seriously injure if not kill herself. If it was her only option, maybe she'd have been able to force herself to try it. But she still hoped to have a chance to talk him out of his murderous plans.

The staircase ended and she stepped with relief onto a solid wood floor. The room was a square tower with three tall arrow slits in each wall. A wrought iron ladder led to a trap door in the ceiling on her left and a chaise lounge and small iron table were positioned directly beneath the set of arrow slits in front of her. The center of the room was empty, although smudges of colored wax stained the wooden planks.

Alaric grabbed her by the shoulders and steered her over to the chaise, pushing her down onto it. The cloak slid off her shoulders to puddle around her hips. "Sit."

Once certain that she would do as he instructed, he ignored her, peering out the arrow slits. She wondered if he was searching for signs of Reynart's imminent return.

Gervaise clumped up the stairs, his arms filled with papers, ropes, rags and an ominous looking dagger. He deposited the load on the tiny table, then hauled Angie to her feet and stuffed one of the rags into her mouth. A second rag bound it in place, cutting cruelly into the corners of her mouth as he knotted it behind her head.

"What's the gag for?" Alaric asked. "You've already taken away her voice."

"For our plan to work, you must bind her power with your blood. Having any other magical bindings in place at the time adds too much risk."

Alaric's face paled as his gaze was drawn to the dagger. "Bound with my blood?"

"Yes. As the blood you gave me was the key to the magic that called her here." The mage's eyes narrowed. "It was your blood you gave me, wasn't it?"

"You just said it had to be blood that was bound to the Nord D'Rae network. You didn't say it had to be mine."

The mage cursed long and fluently, while Alaric's face turned redder and redder, until she thought he was in danger of exploding. Finally, Gervaise took a deep breath and stopped swearing.

"What's done is done. She's here and her power is yet unbound. But before you can bind it, you will need to make it receptive to you. I suggest the same method your brother has been using."

Alaric's hot gaze traveled down the length of her bare legs. Angie trembled, gathering her resolve for one last effort to fight him off. She couldn't use her hands but she could still kick him where it would be most effective.

She glanced at his face, expecting to see triumph at finally taking something of Reynart's. Instead, his blue eyes were clouded and he was biting his lip.

Softly, he said, "But I'm not my brother, am I?"

Angie's heart leaped with hope. Alaric was not so far gone to decency that he would force himself upon an unwilling woman. They'd find another way to reach her power, like using her blood. That possibility would have terrified her a few minutes ago but now she welcomed the alternative.

Gervaise snarled. "We have conspired to commit treason. If we're discovered, we're both dead. With excruciatingly painful deaths. Are you willing to die for her sensibilities?"

Alaric flushed. "Of course not."

"Then what are you waiting for?"

"I…I'm too nervous. I can't…"

Gervaise muttered under his breath, then asked, "Can you at least hold her?"

"I…"

Gervaise glared at the prince.

"Yes. I can. But how will that—?"

"It does not matter which of us breaks Prince Reynart's claim on her power. Once his claim is broken, I can bind you to her power using the same spell that binds you to the gateways."

"But that spell can only be performed on infants! It would destroy an adult."

"I have labored these past years to bring you to power. Why would I now destroy you? Her magic is nowhere near as strong as the gateways. You are in no danger. Although it would be easiest if you claimed her directly."

Alaric shook his head.

"Then raise her skirts."

Alaric untied her belt, letting it fall unheeded to the floor. He gathered the fabric of her chemise and Reynart's old tunic in his hands, his damp palms brushing her thighs and hips as he pushed the cloth up to her chest, baring her body to Gervaise's eager gaze.

Her legs shook but she forced herself to remain still. He had to release the spell holding her arms before he could rape her or his magic wouldn't work correctly. That would be her best chance to get free. She had to act complacent until then, so they would not be prepared for her attack.

Alaric circled behind her and grabbed her upper arms, his fingers digging deep into her flesh as he hauled her backward and braced her body against his.

"I'm releasing the binding spells," Gervaise warned. He didn't say anything or make any gestures but suddenly Angie's arms pulled backward in Alaric's grasp. Screaming as loudly as she could beneath the gag, she wriggled and squirmed, trying to break his hold, but had no success. She kicked back, striking a glancing blow off his shin. Alaric grunted. Then he released one of her arms and grabbed her tightly around the chest, pinning her against his body. With his other hand, he smacked her on the side of the head.

Angie slumped in his grasp, the world dimming around her. Unlike Katya, she wasn't killed by the blow. Watching Gervaise unfasten his red velvet trous, she wasn't sure if she should be pleased to have escaped Katya's fate or not. She didn't think she had the strength to fight him off. But she might not have to wait for them to kill her. Given the way her head was spinning, she was in real danger of throwing up and, with the gag in her mouth, if she did, she'd suffocate.

Chapter Nine

Reynart crouched over Hurricane's neck, giving the stallion his head, as he did every time he rode him. This was the secret to his control of the horse. Hurricane loved to run and Reynart loved the freedom and potential for escape that riding the horse gave him. Never mind that such freedom was illusory. Even if all he wanted was to get away, the King would fear that he was raising an army or using his magical connection to the gateway network to help invaders. To leave the royal court was to be declared a traitor and sentenced to death.

He bent closer, urging Hurricane to greater speed, the horse's warm fur brushing against his cheek with every thrust and return of his powerful neck. Hurricane had quickly learned that he could only run when Reynart was riding him and Reynart never tried to control his initial burst of speed. After that first heady run, the horse was amenable to course or speed corrections. But first, he had to make up for all the days this week when he hadn't run.

They thundered through the old mustering grounds, the flat plain behind the castle where former kings had encamped their standing armies. Now it was occupied by tents once a year for the Grand Fair but otherwise it was a flat stretch of grassland perfect for a horse eager to stretch his legs.

Reynart nudged the horse lightly with his knee and Hurricane veered toward the left, away from the royal hunting preserve, and towards the farmland outside of Dalthar. This was the first time Reynart had been on a horse since his disciplining and, as always, his first reaction was a desire to run as far and as fast as he could, to find a place outside of the King's reach. Somewhere he could live without always watching over his shoulder and weighing every word.

But the dream held little appeal today. Instead, his thoughts drifted back to the castle, wondering what Anjeli was doing and wishing he'd been able to spend the morning making love to her as they'd both desired.

His time with her this week had been sweet, a stolen idyll. But he'd known it couldn't last. He no longer had any reason to stay in his rooms all day and he couldn't endanger her safety by acting in a way that would draw attention to her hiding place. He hoped Ladria might find a way for them to still be together, either inside the castle or meeting discreetly in the city. But even so, it would not be the same as living with her, spending hours in her company. And there was always the danger that Anjeli would not want to remain. She loved him but that was not enough to keep her here. She loved her parents as well. And Reynart had nothing to offer her, except the possibility of one day ruling Nord D'Rae, if his father didn't kill him first.

That thought led to thoughts of the Queen's attempt on his life, via Darvell. The young nobleman had been constantly watched by two of his father's private guards, who would continue to watch him until they delivered him to the baron's estate. He was being sent home in disgrace to lick his wounds and Reynart would have no opportunity to question him. Unless he created the opportunity.

He could poison the two guards. The poison didn't need to be fatal. A simple sleeping draught would suffice, or something that would make them too ill to defend their charge. But how could he deliver the poison without being caught, and without accidentally dosing Darvell with it as well?

Hurricane's galloping charge shifted to a more cautious trot as they approached the edge of the grassland. Reynart guided him to one of the many paths that snaked through the farmland, this one weaving between fields of grain and hillsides covered in grape vines.

Once on the path, Hurricane resumed his gallop, although he wasn't running as quickly as he had been. Soon, Reynart would be able to drop him back down to a trot.

In the meantime, Reynart puzzled over which poison would be best to use. Eventually, he concluded that tincture of Valerian would suit his needs. The question now was how to deliver it.

He straightened up, leaning back in the saddle. Hurricane slowed to a canter, but was not yet willing to end his run. The path was clear ahead of them, so Reynart let him run.

By the time Reynart had considered and discarded a dozen methods of administering the poison as being too liable for him to get caught, or too uncertain of getting the correct dose, Hurricane had slowed to a trot. They were well into the farm country, now, and approaching one of the tiny clusters of buildings that formed the first ring of villages surrounding Dalthar.

Hurricane stopped at the banks of the stream marking the boundary of the village, then cautiously forded through the slow-moving water.

It must have been wash day, because all the women of the village were turned out, pounding clothing against the rocks and scrubbing it with coarse laundry soap. Bubbles floated and danced down the stream.

Reynart's attention was caught by a thin stream of red in the water, the bubbles surrounding it stained pink. His shock communicated itself to Hurricane and the horse stopped in the middle of the stream, water flowing around his fetlocks.

The elderly woman washing the bloody garment glanced up, meeting Reynart's eyes. She turned away, her gaze taking in all of the other village women, then glanced back at him, her eyes filled with sadness.

His blood ran cold. Surely this was a coincidence. Farmers were just as likely as noblemen to have accidents resulting in bloodstained clothing, more likely when you considered they also slaughtered farm animals. It was not surprising that one woman's laundry had bloodstains. It was surprising that more of them did not.

The reasoned argument did nothing to convince him. When the woman nodded and returned to her scrubbing, he was certain his fear was correct. The Amin-Te had appeared to him. He was going to die.

Ignoring the risk of uncertain footing, he turned Hurricane in the middle of the stream, and splashed back the way they'd come. He had to get back to the castle. If someone was going to kill him, he had to make sure Anjeli was safe first.

He urged Hurricane into a fast canter, doubting the horse would have the energy to gallop all the way back but wanting to return as quickly as he could. As he rode, he continued telling himself that he was no hero of legend, and he was undeserving of a visit from the Amin-Te. It had just been a strange coincidence.

His heart refused to believe anything other than that Anjeli was in danger, and that he must return to the castle. Now. The race back to the castle passed in a blur. Hurricane's coat was flecked with sweat but he was still running easily and not blowing.

Reynart dismounted in the courtyard, throwing the reins to one of the stable boys.

"Walk him until he cools, then rub him down and feed him a mash," he ordered. He patted Hurricane on the shoulder, then strode briskly into the castle.

As soon as he was out of the public spaces, he stepped up his pace to a quick jog, hurrying back to his rooms.

He grabbed the doorknob, and had already twisted it open before the odd feel of it registered. There was no tingle of magic, raising the hair on his skin and pricking him like tiny needles. His wards had been destroyed.

He opened the door a crack and checked the crossbow trap. Still deactivated. Sparing a thought for other possible traps that might be the cause of his imminent death, but unwilling to waste the time that would be required to look for them, he threw open the door and ran inside.

"Anjeli!" he called.

No answer. Shattered glass and pottery littered the shelves, sprayed outward from the former wards, and the table had been overturned, as if knocked over in a fight. He looked in his bedroom. The armoire door hung open, with three mismatched shoes spilled on the floor in front of it.

Only a powerful mage could have breached the magical wards his sister had given him. And in the entire city of Dalthar, only one mage had the political power to risk Reynart's anger. Gervaise had found Anjeli at last.

Reynart cursed under his breath, consigning Gervaise to Amin-Ra's most evil and untimely of deaths, and begging that he be allowed to strike the deathblow, then in the next breath bargaining for clemency if only Anjeli was unharmed. But as he swore, he ran back out into the hallway, then turned and sprinted toward the mage's chambers. He'd never been more thankful of the King's paranoia, which insisted his valued advisor and potentially deadliest enemy be kept close at hand.

He wrapped his hand in the hem of his tunic and grabbed the knob. Ignoring the fire that blazed across his skin, he wrenched open the door.

From upstairs, he heard a woman's muffled scream, suddenly silenced. Anjeli!

He ran up the spiral staircase, blanking his mind of everything but an ongoing analysis of his tactical condition, his position and the weapons he had available. The effort took everything he had and only years of the King's harsh lessons allowed him to bury the dictates of his heart. Even so, it was harder to create the necessary distance than any protective shell he'd ever made. But he was going into battle and there was no room for emotion.

He entered the tower room behind Gervaise, whose trous were around his ankles. Anjeli lay before him on the chaise, the tunic she wore as a dress pushed up around her ribs, while another man pinned her to the couch.

He grabbed Gervaise and pulled him away from Anjeli, hurling him toward the far wall. Years of military strategy urged him to follow the threat, to confirm that Gervaise was neutralized. But all he saw was Anjeli, blinking and squinting to focus on him. She said something beneath her gag, the words indistinguishable, but the tone broken.

"Anjeli," he breathed.

The man holding her released her arms and started to rise. Reynart grabbed her, pulling her off the couch and to her feet, then swinging her around and urging her toward the stairs as he interposed his body between her and Gervaise's assistant.

Anjeli wrenched off her gag and turned to face him. Her eyes widened and she gasped, "He has a knife!"

Reynart heard a footstep behind him and instinctively knelt, released his first knife and threw toward the sound.

It wasn't Gervaise. It was his assistant. But for the first time, Reynart could see his face.

He froze, staring at his brother. "Alaric?"

Alaric's left hand rose to his chest, clutching the silver handle of the dagger. His blue eyes widened and he grabbed a tiny wrought iron table with his other hand. The table tipped over with a clatter, spilling papers across the floor, and Alaric fell to his knees.

"Rey?" he gasped.

Reynart knelt beside him, gathering his brother in his arms. "Ric. I'm sorry. I'm so sorry. I didn't know it was you."

Alaric sucked in a burbling breath. "Hurts…"

Reynart pressed his fingers to the wound in Alaric's chest, his brother's hot blood welling up around the blade and over his hand. Bubbling blood. The blade had nicked a lung.

"You're not going to die." He turned, looking for Gervaise. The Pair-forsaken mage could fix this and do at least one good thing with his miserable life.

Angie stared in horror as Reynart clutched his dying brother, the two calling each other by nicknames they probably hadn't used since they were children. Her vision was still swimming, the princes splitting into four, then reuniting into two, over and over again. She pulled down her tunic and chemise, covering as much of her legs as she could. That made her feel slightly more secure but the room continued eddying threateningly around her. She clutched the stone wall beside her and stepped away from the dangerously swaying stairs.

Ignored by the two brothers, Gervaise struggled to his feet and pulled up his fallen trous. He glared at Reynart's back, then winced and clapped his hand to his head, as if he, too, was suffering from double vision. Staggering across the room, he approached Angie.

She tried to focus on him but he kept multiplying and dividing, so she wasn't sure which of him was the real mage. She'd have thought it was a clever magic trick, except the windows behind him were doing the same thing, so she knew it was an aftereffect of the blow to the head Alaric had given her.

She closed her eyes. When he tried to finish what he'd started, she'd only get one chance to hit him. She couldn't trust her eyes but that didn't matter. He'd have to touch her. She'd just swing at whichever one of him touched her.

His labored breathing drew near her and she tensed, anticipating a grab. Instead, he shouldered her aside and sent her sprawling to the floor.

She looked up to see him clattering down the stairs.

Reynart turned, looking around the room, his green eyes wide in his white face. "Gervaise! Where are you? Pair forsake you, mage, Alaric needs you!"

Angie crawled to Reynart's side, avoiding his bleeding brother. She swallowed twice to find her voice, then whispered, "He ran away."

"You let him go?" Reynart glared at her. "How could you?"

She clutched her throbbing head. "But he's gone. Isn't that good?"

"No." Reynart's voice broke and he turned back to his brother, clasping Alaric's fingers in his bloody hand. "He's gone, Ric. I can't heal it."

Alaric's fingers tightened briefly, and Reynart squeezed his brother's hand. With his other hand, he reached up and brushed his brother's blond hair away from his face, smearing blood across his forehead and into his hair.

"I didn't know it was you," he whispered, his voice cracking. "I didn't know."

"Rey…" Alaric breathed wetly.

Reynart bent forward to hear his whispered words but Alaric only gasped for air, coughed out a mouthful of blood and sagged limply in his arms.

"No!" Reynart screamed. His forehead pressed to Alaric's, he rocked his brother's limp body back and forth. But Alaric was beyond comforting.

Angie bit her lip, completely at a loss for what to do. If she stopped to think, to realize what had almost happened, what would have happened if Reynart hadn't arrived to save her, she'd start screaming and never stop. Or maybe she'd just throw up. The way the world kept shifting and flowing around her, throwing up was looking like a better and better option all the time.

But Reynart had also just killed his brother. Never mind that Alaric had grabbed the dagger off the table, and would have stabbed Reynart in the back with it if she hadn't warned him. He was still Reynart's brother and he'd loved him.

"Reynart?" she asked softly.

He did not answer, continuing to rock his brother's body.

"Reynart!" She reached out and tapped him on the shoulder, ready to leap backwards if he drew a knife on her. But he didn't. He merely lifted his bloodied and tear-streaked face and stared up at her from glassy green eyes, even as he continued gently rocking back and forth.

"You can't collapse now," she insisted. "What about Gervaise? He might have gone for help. The guard could be arriving any moment."

"The Pair-forsaken mage ran away," Reynart growled, his words barely intelligible. "He led Alaric to this pass, then abandoned him in his time of need."

"Yes." Better to have him blaming Gervaise than blaming himself. "And he might come back at any moment. We need to get out of here. I don't know why he didn't use magic against you but he has a spell that can pin your arms to your sides so you can't fight. We have to leave before he comes back, before he gets a chance to finish the job."

"He will tell no one. He cannot, without revealing he left Alaric to die. I will not leave my brother."

Angie knelt on the floor beside him. He might not be afraid of Gervaise but she knew he was afraid of the King. "Reynart, what is the penalty for killing a royal prince?"

He blinked, looking around the tower room as if seeing it for the first time, then glancing down at his brother's body and his black knife buried to the hilt in his chest. He wrenched the blade free, then wiped it clean on his already bloody tunic.

"That's too distinctive. I can't leave the knife."

He scanned the room again, then spotted Gervaise's silver dagger among the litter of papers that had fallen from the table. He grabbed it, shivering as his hand brushed the pages. Then he thrust the dagger into Alaric's wound, making it look as if Gervaise's dagger had killed him.

Tentatively, he picked up the scattered pages, glancing at each sheet briefly as he did.

"To ensure succession. To hamper pursuit. To invoke power." He shook his head. "They all make my skin itch, the way Ladria's magic does when I help her. Gervaise must have readied all of these spells with his power, and was just waiting for Alaric's assistance to use the gateway magic for additional power."

"Yes. He said something about that. Something about aligning energy. No, attuning energy. That was it."

Reynart frowned at the top sheet of paper, spattered with his brother's blood. "But then these spells should have been invoked. The power to do so rests in the blood. Unless Gervaise feared invoking them in the wrong order? Maybe the text also needed to be read."

"Maybe." She wasn't quite sure what she was agreeing to. Her thoughts were occupied with not throwing up but the more she thought about not doing it, the more her body seemed to want to vomit. She gripped Reynart's shoulder, seeking an oasis of stability.

"I open the power of the gateways, through a network of space, calling magical forces to me, for my use, and my bidding," he read, then snorted. "Those aren't even the right words to invoke the gateways."

A wave of nausea passed over Angie and she fell to the floor. Closing her eyes, she concentrated with all her being on breathing in, then breathing out.

A moment later, Reynart was shaking her shoulder, rousing her to awareness.

"You fainted. Come on. I have to get you out of here, away from the castle. I read the spell to discourage pursuit, just in case it works. But we need to leave before anyone discovers what has happened."

He gathered her in his arms, then stood up. She clutched him around the neck but the world seemed to have stopped spinning. Perhaps passing out briefly had helped.

"Grab my cloak from the chaise," he ordered. "Your hands are clean."

No, they weren't. But the bloodstains on her hands weren't the sort that could be seen by anyone else. She could have used Alaric's name when warning Reynart.

She'd known how he would react. Had she been purposefully vague because she wanted Alaric to suffer for his part in her near rape? But she hadn't wanted him dead. Even if some part of her had, she never would have wanted his death to be at Reynart's hand.

She reached out and obligingly grabbed the cloak.

"Hold on."

She closed her eyes and clutched him tightly, burying her face in his neck as he carried her down the narrow spiral stairs. The room below looked like a whirlwind had passed through it.

Reynart set her on her feet. "Can you stand?"

"I think so." She swayed a bit, but remained upright.

"Good. Put on the cloak. Pull it tight around you."

He started toward Gervaise's bedroom and terror nearly stole her voice again. She squeaked, "Where are you going?"

"I need a cloak to cover myself. These bloodstains would be noticed."

She looked at him, finally able to focus well enough to really see him. His hose were soaked with blood, as were the knees of his trous. His tunic was spattered across the chest and smeared at the hem and sleeves.

Then her gaze lifted to his face. It was completely expressionless. Blood smeared his forehead and the tracks of his tears still shone on his cheeks. But his eyes no longer held grief, or remorse, or even fear for their possible capture. They were as flat and as dead as his brother's sightless gaze.

He was going into shock. Her fear tried to rouse her with another spurt of adrenaline but her beleaguered body had given all it had to give. She'd trusted that Reynart would save her. But if he shut down and gave up, they were both doomed.

"What do you need?" she asked, hoping to keep him thinking, keep him actively involved in their escape.

"A cloak. Gervaise is almost my height. It would disguise me well enough for the walk back to my chambers."

She nodded. "I'll wait here."

He disappeared into Gervaise's bedroom. She used the time to shake out the cloak she'd worn earlier and wrap it around her shoulders. Reynart returned a short time later wrapped in a cloak of dark green wool with a fur collar. It accented the flatness of his eyes.

"Can you walk?" he asked.

"Yes."

"Then follow me. Say nothing."

Silently, she followed him out of the mage's suite, down the hall and around the corner to the private wing of the castle. The guard at the far end, in front of the King's rooms, watched as they crossed to Reynart's door, opened it and went inside.

Once inside, Reynart threw off Gervaise's borrowed cloak and quickly stripped out of his bloodied clothing. He walked into the bedroom and she heard the sounds of water being poured into a basin, then the opening and closing of doors and drawers in the armoire.

When he came back into the sitting room, he was dressed in a tunic of dark green leather with velvet sleeves and embellishments around the neck, green leather trous, and tall black riding boots. The dark green cloak matched perfectly.

He was also carrying her gown and a pair of leather saddlebags. "Take off that tunic and put your gown back on. I'll lace it for you."

She grabbed the tunic by the hem and lifted it, suffering a brief flashback of Alaric doing the same thing. But she couldn't afford to give in to her fears now. They were not yet safe.

She tossed the tunic away and raised her arms so that Reynart could put the gown over her head. He held it while she slipped her arms into the sleeves, then quickly did up the laces, tightening them until she could barely breathe. He swung his cloak around her shoulders, and steered her toward the door.

"One more thing." He crossed to his shelves and swept most of the contents into the saddle bag, leaving only the shattered containers that had held the door wards and a square wooden box. Opening the box, he revealed a silver circlet resting on a bed of velvet. He placed the circlet on his head, pulling his hair over it to hide it, then slung the saddlebags over his shoulder.

"Let's go."

She followed him out into the hallway, down the stairs and into a part of the castle she'd never seen before. They passed servants, who all bowed or curtseyed to Reynart as he walked by, and well-dressed men and women who nodded their heads and eyed her with speculation. He ignored them all.

A young nobleman stepped in front of him, blocking his path. "Moving your things out to the stables, are you?"

There was a collective indrawn breath of all the other courtiers in the hall, who instantly discovered other places they urgently needed to be. In the time it took Reynart to stop and look the nobleman up and down, the hall emptied.

"Get out of my way, Olivier."

"Prince Alaric told me all about your assignment for the King. A handful of rebellious peasants are no match for a nobly-commanded army, although of course you'd like to think commoners stood a chance. In a few candlemarks, he'll be the rightful heir and you'll be nothing."

Reynart took a deep breath. "Get out of my way, Olivier. I do not have the patience for witless sparring with you today."

His black knife appeared in his hand, the movement drawing Olivier's gaze. The young nobleman glanced around the corridor, as if seeking support, his eyes widening as he realized he'd been abandoned.

Lifting his jaw, Olivier announced, "Dueling inside the castle is illegal."

Reynart's lips turned in a feral approximation of a smile. "It would not be a duel."

The remaining color drained from Olivier's face and he swallowed audibly. His gaze settled on Angie, no doubt worried about where she fit in the political structure.

She smiled pleasantly, and moved a half step closer to Reynart, clearly signaling her loyalties.

"You're not worth the effort," Olivier sneered, then turned and swept down the hall far faster than he had approached.

Reynart's hand tightened on the knife and he lifted his arm, then shook his head and sheathed the blade.

They saw other courtiers and servants on the way to the stables but no one else tried to stop them. As they walked across the open courtyard to the stables, Reynart asked, "Can you ride by yourself?"

"No." She'd never even been on a horse.

"My horse will have to carry us both. Let us pray Amin-Ra is satisfied with the sacrifice he has already received this day and the spell to confound pursuit works. We cannot afford to announce our intention to take a long journey by calling for a fresh horse. And I will not leave him here, to be mistreated and abused in my absence."

A boy ran up to them, bowing to Reynart. "My lord Prince, your horse is still cooling down."

Reynart blinked. "So little time has passed?"

"Not even half a candlemark, my lord Prince. And we would not rush our duty."

"Commendable." He pulled the saddlebags off of his shoulder and held them out to the boy. "Saddle Hurricane again. His other saddle will be dry."

The boy frowned, and pointed at the dark gray clouds scudding in from the east. "There's a storm coming."

"I am aware of that. Saddle my horse."

The boy gulped and bowed. "Yes, my lord Prince."

A few minutes later, the boy reappeared leading a massive reddish-brown horse. The color of his coat reminded Angie of bloodstains and she focused on her breathing, fighting to forget what she'd just seen, or at least put off thinking about it until she was someplace safe.

The boy led the horse next to a set of wooden steps and Reynart nudged her to follow and climb the stairs.

From the top step, the saddle was at the level of her hips. The boy circled the horse and grabbed the stirrup on the far side, while Reynart stood on the ground beside the steps holding out the near stirrup.

"Put your left foot in and hop up, then turn to sit sideways."

Clumsily, she put her foot in the stirrup, which lurched alarmingly as she put her weight on it. The stable boy grunted with effort as he counterbalanced her by pulling on the opposing stirrup.

"Good," Reynart said. "Now turn and sit on the pommel. It will be uncomfortable but you won't be there for long."

She followed his orders, terrified that the horse would bounce into motion, tossing her to the ground. The cobblestones of the courtyard seemed very far away and painfully hard.

Reynart walked the horse a step forward, then slipped her foot from the stirrup and replaced it with his own. With one hand he grabbed the saddle beneath her hip, grabbing the back of the saddle with his other hand. His leg muscles flexed as his arms pulled and he sprang neatly into the saddle.

He found the other stirrup with the toe of his boot, then pulled her across his lap, settling her weight over the center of the saddle. Gathering the reins in his hands, he squeezed the horse's sides with his legs, and the horse stepped forward.

The stable boy tried to dissuade them one last time. "My lord Prince, this storm looks like a bad one. If someone needs to be sent after you, where should I tell them to look?"

"You may tell them we have gone into the city, and will be taking shelter at an inn should the storm prevent our return."

The boy looked as if he didn't believe that answer, but knew better than to argue. Instead, he bowed. "As you will it, my lord Prince."

They left the courtyard and circled around the castle toward a large open field behind it. Angie slid her arms beneath Reynart's cloak and held him tightly.

"Relax. They will not pursue us for at least a candlemark. By then, we will be through the nearest gateway, to the outpost on Kingscap."

The first fat raindrops spattered them, miniature water bombs of cold and discomfort. Angie turned her face away, burying it in the thick fur collar of Reynart's cloak.

Closing her eyes, she relaxed into the gentle rocking gait of the horse and allowed Reynart's quiet strength to support her. "I was so afraid," she whispered.

He took one of his hands away from the reins to hug her briefly, almost impersonally, but said nothing. She needed to talk about her experience, to air her fears and worries so that they lost their power over her. But not yet. Because then he would have to face what he had done and she needed him to remain the cold, emotionless person he had become. Once he got them to safety, then they could talk.

So she hugged him close and tried to reassure him with her body, as she could not do with words.

The rain continued to fall, turning the farmland they rode through into a misty dreamscape, punctuated by occasional glimpses of fields of grain, farmhouses or grape vines. The wheel ruts in the track they followed were soon filled with water, the horse kicking up plumes of spray with every step. Reynart's body tensed and he looked carefully around them.

"This is not natural. I've never seen so much rain outside of a hurricane, yet there is no wind."

"Won't it make it harder for anyone to follow our trail?"

"I'm more concerned about the gateway. It's in a low spot. If there is a flood, it may be unreachable."

Angie shivered. Could this day get any worse? "You said it was the nearest gateway. That means there's another one we can use, right?"

"Yes." He did not relax. "But most of them are in low lying areas."

"But not all?"

"Not all."

"Then if the nearest gateway is flooded, we will aim for one on high ground."

Reynart nodded silently.

They arrived at the gateway, or what Angie assumed was the gateway. A broad square of stone surrounded a pair of stone pillars. Water covered the square half a foot deep.

Reynart steered the horse to the pillars, then reached out and rested his hand against one.

"Dead," he said, his voice completely toneless. "We ride to the next."

The second and third gateways were also flooded. Angie began to shiver, soaked to the skin and cramped from the hours on horseback. The horse also seemed to be tiring, his once proud and alert head now bobbing numbly with his steps, his ears folded back instead of swiveling to catch the slightest sound.

Of course, there was nothing to hear except the rain and the splash of his hooves through the water.

Reynart hesitated a moment and the horse dropped his head, blowing gustily. Then he snapped the reins, pulling the horse's head back up, and turned him off of the track.

"We'll take a short cut."

Angie lifted her face from the fur collar of his cloak to study the rough path carved into the hillside that he was urging the horse upon. A muddy waterfall coursed over the path, awash with sticks and leaves.

"Is it safe? Maybe we should take the long way."

"The water is too high. If we take the long way, this gateway will be flooded, too. And it's the last one."

Biting her lip, she burrowed deeper into his cloak. He held her close, his steady strength reassuring her that he would get them to safety.

The horse stumbled, his hooves slipping on the muddy path. Angie's waterlogged skirts weighed her down, threatening to pull her from her precarious perch across Reynart's lap, and she clutched him in terror. She didn't want to die.

His arm tightened around her waist, holding her securely, and he shifted his weight, mutely instructing the horse to stop. The horse obeyed instantly, lowering his head, his sides heaving with great, shuddering breaths. He shifted restlessly from hoof to hoof, pulling first one then another from the fetlock-deep sucking mud that threatened to glue him to the hillside if he remained still.

Reynart loosened the ties of his cloak, pulling it around her, adding another layer of wet wool to the sopping clothing that was leaching all warmth from her skin. His leather and velvet clad chest was mostly dry and radiated warmth and she snuggled closer, shivering, as she tried to absorb his heat. Beneath her cheek, his heart beat steadily. She listened to the sound in amazement. After all he had been through today, and despite their current precarious situation, he showed no fear.

She didn't understand it. She was a mess, simply from what might have been. How much worse for him, who had mistakenly killed his beloved younger brother? He'd been forced to flee his home and, if they were caught, she was certain the King would torture him to death. Or possibly torture and heal him over and over again in a sadistic cycle that would not end until Reynart's abused body finally could not take any more.

Her tears mingled with the rain trickling down from her sodden hair and she clutched Reynart tightly around the chest. Fear for him overwhelmed her, driving away all thoughts of her own fears.

He gave the signal to his horse and the beast reluctantly started moving again. The water was so high now that every step threw plumes of muddy water against her dangling legs, drenching her already soaked skirts. But neither the horse nor his master would give up.

Eventually, they reached the final gateway.

Water slicked the stone surrounding the stone pillars and colored lights flickered ominously between them, like a light bulb about to burn out. Reynart urged his horse into a stumbling run.

The horse slipped as his hooves struck the wet stone, but recovered after a heart-stopping lurch, and thundered through the opening.

Light crackled around them, then they were floating, drifting in a cloud of shifting, drifting streamers of color. The sound of rain, a constant companion for hours, suddenly stilled. Angie closed her eyes, burrowing beneath Reynart's cloak. His heart beat steadily and she focused on that sound, on the feel of his warm chest beneath her cheek, on his arm wrapped securely around her waist.

The horse lurched again, his hooves striking mud and sliding before he recovered his balance. Reynart's arm tightened around her, holding her fast on the stumbling horse.

"You can open your eyes now," he said.

Hesitantly, she pulled her head out from under his cloak and looked around with wide eyes. They were on a hillside overlooking a bustling port town, the Mediterranean-styled homes with whitewashed walls and clay tiled roofs nothing like the stone buildings of Nord D'Rae. More obviously, the evening sun beat down from a cloudless blue sky, parching the ground everywhere except the puddle of water flowing out from between the carved pillars behind them.

The orange light between the pillars sparked one last time, then vanished. The existing water flowed past the horse's hooves, rolling down the hillside, and no new water took its place.

"Where are we?" she whispered.

"The Empire of Illornia."

* * * * *

Reynart found them accommodations at an inn that was clean enough to pose no health risk but shady enough to ask no questions of their patrons. They fell into an exhausted sleep, barely able to believe that they were finally safe.

He woke in the middle of the night from a dream of his brother. For a moment, he thought it was all a dream. Then he remembered.

His heart shattered.

"No," he moaned. If he added up the pain from all the years he had taken the King's displeasure upon himself, shielding his younger brother the only way he knew how, it would be as nothing compared to the agony suffusing him now.

His arms tightened around Anjeli, blindly seeking comfort, and she tensed in her sleep. He released her and rolled away, his chest gripped by a giant's crushing fist so that he could hardly breathe.

He had failed her, as well. Over and over again, he had promised to protect her, to keep her safe. Instead, he had allowed Gervaise to steal her away. That she hadn't been raped was merely an indication of the Heavenly Pair's divine mercy and no reflection upon his skill. She would never trust his word again. He did not deserve her trust.

A strangled cry escaped him, like a wounded animal caught in a death trap. He knew how to withstand torture and abuse, retreating into the corners of his mind where the King's discipline had never been able to reach. But there was no escape from the pain that consumed him now. And no end to it. He could not recant, or apologize, or pledge a new behavior. Nothing could ever make right what he had done.

Then Anjeli shifted, rolling over and rising up on one elbow to gaze down at him. "I wondered when you were going to start feeling again."

Disbelieving, he twisted his head and dared to look at her. He saw no condemnation, no disgust. Only concern, for him. And…could it be possible? Love?

Hesitantly, she reached out to him, putting her arm lightly around him, as if she feared he might push her away. Him! When she deserved to flog him to within an inch of his life for his failures. Flog him to death, if she willed it. Yet she showed no interest in punishing him for his crimes.

Struggling to breathe, he reached tentatively toward her, unable to believe that she could be so forgiving. Surely he must be misinterpreting her gesture.

Her arms closed around him in a savage hug, pulling him to her and crushing his face to her breasts while she wrapped herself around him as if she'd never let him go. The last restraints on his emotions burst and he gasped for breath, shuddering and quaking like an ancient suffering from palsy. Fiercely, he clutched her, too, burrowing his face between her breasts.

"I'm sorry. I'm so sorry I failed you."

"You didn't fail me." She stroked his hair and his back, soothing him, until finally he could breathe again.

He gulped in a huge lungful of air, and continued his confession. "My sister will not be able to find us here. You are trapped in this world you loathe."

She tightened her arms around him, and kissed his temple. "But I'll be with you."

He didn't know what else to say. He deserved to be punished but she was determined not to punish him.

His voice broke. "How can you forgive me? I killed my own brother!"

"Because I love you. And because he would have killed you if you hadn't."

"You can't know that."

"I saw him pick up the knife."

"But you don't know why. What if he only meant to threaten with it, to allow himself to escape? Or what if he had come to his senses, and meant to attack Gervaise?" Another broken cry squeezed itself from his chest and he hid his face in Anjeli's warmth, unable to see her expression. "I never gave him a chance."

"He broke into your rooms, looking for your troop analysis. He was planning on cheating, since he couldn't beat you fairly."

"Arranging pieces on a chess board. That's not the same—"

"He and Gervaise spent three years working on the spells to eliminate you and the King."

"Gervaise wanted Alaric as King. He wrote the spells. Alaric had no hand in that plot."

"What would convince you that he'd meant to kill you? If he'd stabbed you in the back?" she countered hoarsely, her arms tightening around him until brilliant bands of blue streaked his vision. "Then held me down so Gervaise could rape me?"

Reynart moaned. The brother he'd known could never have done that. But that's exactly what he had been doing. Reynart had to believe his brother would have repented and stopped Gervaise, if Reynart had not arrived to save Anjeli. That Alaric would have found the courage to stand up for what was right. But because of him, his brother had never gotten the chance to be a hero.

"Forgive me," he begged, not sure if he wanted Anjeli's forgiveness, Alaric's, or the Heavenly Pair's. He didn't deserve it from any of them. But maybe, if they forgave him, this pain would end.

"You saved me," she whispered. "Now let me save you."

She rolled him onto his back and straddled him. Taking his face firmly in her hands, she kissed each of his eyelids, then pressed a deep, cleansing kiss on his lips.

"I love you," she repeated. "You are someone worth loving."

His mind still struggled to believe her but his body responded without hesitation. Wrapping his arms around her, he drew her down on top of him and melted into her kiss.

She was his lodestone, inexorably drawing him to her, and he would be lost without her. His lifelong quest to be recognized as the rightful heir to the crown was meaningless now. Perhaps, if he had stayed, the blame for Alaric's death would not have fallen on him. Even if it had, as the King's sole remaining non-magical child, he might have survived. But Anjeli would have been destroyed, brutally and publicly.

That could not be allowed to happen. He had sworn to protect her and he would, regardless of the cost. She was all that was important now.

"I love you, Anjeli."

She smiled against his lips. "Then shut up and do something about it."

Slowly, he loosened the laces of her dress until the sweet perfection of her breasts swung free. He kissed the creamy upper curves of each soft mound, then stroked her nipples with his tongue.

She moaned softly, flexing her hips against his and rousing his spear to battle readiness.

"Take me, Reynart. Make me forget."

A sharp pain lanced his heart and he closed his eyes briefly to stave off the blow. Perhaps he would find forgetfulness in her arms, as well. She offered forgiveness, too, but he was unwilling to accept it, unable to forgive himself. Forgetfulness, for however short a time, was the next best thing.

Gently, he lifted her chemise and dress up over her head, baring her body. She shivered in the faint chill of the room, her skin rising in gooseflesh. He briskly rubbed her back and arms, heating her with his touch, then drew the discarded blanket over them to trap their bodies' warmth.

She sighed softly. "You are still fully clothed. That doesn't seem fair."

He rolled her onto her side, hesitant to place her beneath him lest the position raise unwelcome memories for her. But he had learned to dress and undress in full battle armor within the cramped environs of a campaign tent. He easily slipped out of his clothing, encumbered only by the blanket.

When they were both naked, he drew her to him again. His hands skimmed her hips and ass, gently fitting her body to his. She sighed softly as his spear slid between her legs but he was in no hurry to enter her. This joining was for her pleasure, as all he did from now on would be for her.

He dusted soft kisses across her shoulders and up the curve of her neck, nuzzling and licking the tender areas beneath her jaw and behind her ears. Anjeli gasped, her fingers tightening on his shoulders, as her hips rocked against his.

Ignoring the increasing urgency of his hardening spear, he stroked her back and feathered her lips with kisses. She moaned against his lips, opening her mouth beneath his and probing with her tongue. He groaned, his spear twitching with eagerness, and devoured her mouth.

He could feel her readiness, the wet heat of her open castle teasing his aching spear. He pulled back slightly, shifting his position, so that the head of his spear pressed against her portcullis. There was no resistance.

Slowly, he pushed forward, slipping beneath her portcullis into the waiting castle beyond. She sighed with pleasure as he slid home, flexing her hips to take him deeper.

The tiny movement undid him, releasing the storm of passion that his fear for her had held in check. He cupped and caressed her hips and ass, thrusting in and out of her, while he kissed her as if he could inhale her very soul.

But it was not enough. He flipped her onto her back, pausing briefly in his onslaught until her clutching fingers urged him to continue. Levering himself up onto his elbows, he used the change in angle to drive deeper, nipping and suckling her breasts as he thrust over and over again.

Anjeli writhed beneath him, moaning his name until she lacked the breath to do more than gasp with pleasure at every deep thrust of his spear, every hard pull of his lips. He was having difficulty holding back his final charge, and reached between their straining bodies to brush his fingers across her swollen barbican.

That was enough to send her over the edge, arching beneath him in a series of shuddering quivers. Her tensing body gripped his spear so tightly he found his own release with hers, groaning in agonized pleasure as he let fly his seed.

Still shivering with the aftermath of their lovemaking, he rolled onto his back, pillowing her body with his own. He held her tightly in his arms as their breathing slowed, their hearts beating a single time. She nestled against his chest, relaxed and at peace.

She had found the forgetfulness she sought but his mind continued to race. Added to his existing worries and concerns was a new one. He had not packed the powder of Ladria's that prevented pregnancies. Even now, Anjeli might have conceived.

He sighed, knowing that a future heir to the throne of Nord D'Rae would complicate their situation far more dangerously than it was now. And yet, if she did conceive a child, the Heavenly Pair would have given their blessing to something he already knew was true. She had been brought from another world for him and he would never find another woman like her. His heart was hers, now and forever.

"Sleep," he whispered, stroking her hair and back in a soothing caress. "I will protect you. You have nothing to fear."

She smiled, snuggling closer, and murmured into his chest, "I've finally found where I belong."

An Excerpt From
FUGITIVE LOVERS

Copyright © JENNIFER DUNNE, 2005.

All Rights Reserved Ellora's Cave Publishing Inc.

Fugitive Lovers

ഔ

Two minutes, six seconds. Raven Armistead shifted into double-time, pounding down the stairs. The last magnesium ribbon fuse had taken too long to light. She should have left it. Now she needed to make up the time, or she wouldn't clear the building before the fire in the data center set off the alarms.

She risked another glance at her digital chronometer. *One minute, fifty-eight seconds.* Less than two minutes until the fuses ignited the blocks of thermite sitting in puddles of water. Then superheated metal droplets would spatter throughout the Inter-Continental Police's data center. Even if half of the fuses went out, the other half would spray enough molten aluminum and iron to destroy all of the computer files the ICP needed to start its roundup. If she'd done everything correctly. She recalled her father's warning, his dry voice reciting her list of past failures, but she resisted the impulse to go back and check. There wasn't time.

Her mission would succeed. It had to.

The Auric Rights League had run out of options. The Auric Rights Bill coming up before the Territorial Congress in a few weeks for a vote would do them no good if the ICP tracked them down and arrested them all first. The ICP interrogators would force the Auric prisoners to admit their powers were gifts of the devil and there'd be no way to save them. Marshall's violent solution sickened her, but she'd do whatever had to be done to protect her people. She wouldn't let the ICP get them.

She passed the second floor. *One minute forty-three seconds left*. Her heart pounded, but the rhythm of her breathing never faltered. The strict regimen of exercises and martial arts training her father forced the team through had paid off. He'd been right to insist on them. As always.

Brilliant green light flashed up the stairwell, blinding her. She grabbed for the banister, her damp palm sliding across the cold steel until she found a secure grip.

Someone had crossed the aura trace she'd left across the building's entrances, and the trail of microscopic crystals reacted to the life force. But who? The building was closed. Only a man in excellent physical condition could cause such an intense flare of color, so it wasn't the flabby security guard returning. The intruder must be an ICP agent working overtime.

Damn her luck. She glanced at her chronometer. *One minute thirty-two seconds*. She had to get down the stairs, across the lobby, outside, across the street, and out of sight before the alarms sounded. If the ICP caught her, they'd use her to uncover League members. They'd force her father to turn himself in. Or maybe he wouldn't ransom her, in which case they'd probably kill her to make an example out of her. She had to get clear.

She thundered down the stairs. First floor. Odds were the agent wouldn't go anywhere near the data center. The computers ran dark, unattended during nights and weekends unless they signaled a problem.

She stopped again, clutching the cold steel banister. Could one of the computer programs have failed, and an automatic call gone out to a service technician? He might be heading toward the data center now, unaware of the maelstrom of boiling metal that would start in one minute twenty-four seconds.

Her father's words burned in her ears. The success of the mission must always come first. Now her indecision supported his belief that she was inept. His first choice, Marshall, would never think of turning back. He'd follow her father's orders to the letter and damn the consequences.

They'd leave the stranger to die. What was one life, compared to the safety of their people? That's what they'd do. But they weren't here. It was up to her to deal with the stranger the way she thought best. ICP agent or unlucky innocent, it didn't matter. Raven had to go back.

She changed direction, pivoting with so much force that her braid flew out and smacked the concrete wall of the stairwell. Pushing her body to its limits, she pelted up the stairs as fast as she could.

Her breath came in gasps, searing her lungs. Every second mattered. Surging up the stairs, she pulled energy from her aura and hoped she'd have enough strength left for a protective shield. She'd never tried a double-shield before. If she miscalculated, she and the stranger would both die. Her father would be furious with her for ruining the mission.

She crashed through the door onto the fifth floor. The hallway was empty, but the steady green of the stranger's aura bled through the open doorway to the computer center. He was already inside. But he might not have reached the room with the explosives.

Slowing her pace only enough to keep from slamming into the walls, she barreled into the empty reception area. The man had already passed into the monitoring room.

She slid her stolen badge through the reader and followed him.

Grabbing a quick breath, she cried out, "Stop right there or I'll call security!"

The man, his clipped brown hair and khaki uniform marking him as an ICP agent, halted in the act of opening the door to the data center. He turned, the easy camaraderie of his dimpled grin at odds with the sudden tension in his body.

"I'm part of the ATS project. I've got authority to be here," he said. "Who are you?"

She looked at her chronometer. *Eight seconds*. A stray spark could set off the explosion at any moment.

"Get away from that door!" Lowering her shoulder, she charged him, sending them both to the ground in a tangle of arms and legs. He struggled to break free of her, but she hugged him tight and rolled to the side, into the shadow of a hulking desk. His head struck the back of the desk, and he lay still.

She pressed close against the agent, the pulse in his neck beating against her cheek. Fear overrode her normal revulsion at being inside the field of another person's aura and she molded herself to him, wrapping one arm around his neck and twining her legs with his.

Heat radiated outward from the center of her groin, pressed against his hip. For a panicked second, she feared that her shield had failed, and a superheated droplet had pierced her flesh, boiling her blood and cooking her internal organs. But her shield was intact. The heat seemed an artifact of their close proximity, and as such, could be safely ignored until the more immediate danger was past.

A tremor ripped through her, from her scalp all the way down to her toes, as her aura tried to align with his. The agent was in prime physical health, lithely muscled, so that laying atop him was like resting upon a sun warmed boulder. Even at rest, his aura vibrated with power, half-blinding her and setting her teeth on edge with the tension. She didn't have the energy to resist him.

About the Author

෩

Jennifer Dunne is the author of over a dozen "Hot and Heartwarming" novels and novellas, with her erotic romances published by Ellora's Cave and her fantasy and science fiction published by Cerridwen Press. A three-time winner of the EPPIE Award, she has been nominated for the PRISM, Sapphire, and Pearl, and won or been nominated for many other awards not named after sparkly gemstones and jewels. To learn more about Jennifer visit her website at www.jenniferdunne.com.

Jennifer welcomes mail from readers. You can write to her c/o Ellora's Cave Publishing at 1056 Home Avenue, Akron OH 44310-3502.

Why an electronic book?

We live in the Information Age—an exciting time in the history of human civilization in which technology rules supreme and continues to progress in leaps and bounds every minute of every hour of every day. For a multitude of reasons, more and more avid literary fans are opting to purchase e-books instead of paperbacks. The question to those not yet initiated to the world of electronic reading is simply: *why?*

1. *Price*. An electronic title at Ellora's Cave Publishing and Cerridwen Press runs anywhere from 40-75% less than the cover price of the <u>exact same title</u> in paperback format. Why? Cold mathematics. It is less expensive to publish an e-book than it is to publish a paperback, so the savings are passed along to the consumer.

2. *Space*. Running out of room to house your paperback books? That is one worry you will never have with electronic novels. For a low one-time cost, you can purchase a handheld computer designed specifically for e-reading purposes. Many e-readers are larger than the average handheld, giving you plenty of screen room. Better yet, hundreds of titles can be stored within your new library—a single microchip. (Please note that Ellora's Cave and Cerridwen Press does not endorse any specific brands. You can check our website at www.ellorascave.com or

www.cerridwenpress.com for customer recommendations we make available to new consumers.)

3. *Mobility.* Because your new library now consists of only a microchip, your entire cache of books can be taken with you wherever you go.

4. *Personal preferences are accounted for.* Are the words you are currently reading too small? Too **large**? Too…**ANNOYING**? Paperback books cannot be modified according to personal preferences, but e-books can.

5. *Instant gratification.* Is it the middle of the night and all the bookstores are closed? Are you tired of waiting days—sometimes weeks—for online and offline bookstores to ship the novels you bought? Ellora's Cave Publishing sells instantaneous downloads 24 hours a day, 7 days a week, 365 days a year. Our e-book delivery system is 100% automated, meaning your order is filled as soon as you pay for it.

Those are a few of the top reasons why electronic novels are displacing paperbacks for many an avid reader. As always, Ellora's Cave and Cerridwen Press welcomes your questions and comments. We invite you to email us at service@ellorascave.com, service@cerridwenpress.com or write to us directly at: 1056 Home Ave. Akron OH 44310-3502.

THE
☥ ELLORA'S CAVE ☥
LIBRARY

Stay up to date with Ellora's Cave Titles in Print with our Quarterly Catalog.

TO RECIEVE A CATALOG,
SEND AN EMAIL WITH YOUR NAME
AND MAILING ADDRESS TO:

CATALOG@ELLORASCAVE.COM

OR SEND A LETTER OR POSTCARD
WITH YOUR MAILING ADDRESS TO:

CATALOG REQUEST
c/o ELLORA'S CAVE PUBLISHING, INC.
1056 HOME AVENUE
AKRON, OHIO 44310-3502

COMING TO A BOOKSTORE NEAR YOU!

ELLORA'S CAVE

Bestselling Authors Tour

UPDATES AVAILABLE AT
WWW.ELLORASCAVE.COM

Ellora's Cavemen
Tales From the Temple

Try an e-book for your immediate
reading pleasure or order these titles in print from

www.EllorasCave.com

Ellora's Cave
The Best in Today's Romantica™

Ellora's Cavemen
Legendary Tails

Try an e-book for your immediate
reading pleasure or order these titles in print from

www.EllorasCave.com

Cerridwen Press

Cerridwen, the Celtic goddess of wisdom, was the muse who brought inspiration to storytellers and those in the creative arts.
Cerridwen Press encompasses the best and most innovative stories in all genres of today's fiction.
Visit our website and discover the newest titles by talented authors who still get inspired—much like the ancient storytellers did…
once upon a time.

www.cerridwenpress.com